Words Catch Fire

GW00455961

Arts Quarter Books

Short Stories, Poems and Photography

Words Catch Fire

Published by

Arts Quarter Books
Teignmouth, Devon

Cover work by Priticreative

ISBN: 9781081194352

Introduction

This book of short stories, poetry and photography is the third in the series from Arts Quarter Books, a Devon based publisher. The title, 'Words Catch Fire', references Gerard Manley Hopkins, 'As kingfishers catch fire, dragonflies draw flame', which inspired me to write a short story a few years ago. At about the same time, Jeanna Dobson wrote what has become our keynote poem.

The recipe for writing success is in this book, but you are needed to decipher it! These short stories and poems include competition winners from three continents and three generations; they fill in the space between us and no reader is left an uninvolved bystander. Even so, they are nothing until you read them!

The winning entries to AQB's Spring 2019 writing competition, 'Closure', by Colleen MacMahon (First Prize) and 'How do I feel about Lentils', by Anna Barker (Second Prize), are featured alongside work by local writers. Given the wide variety of subjects, styles and form, everyone will find something that appeals.

I would like to thank everyone who submitted work for consideration. Unfortunately, it is not possible to publish all the excellent work received.

I would like to thank Rolande Burrows, Gwynneth Chubb, Jill Harrison and Robert Swann for their expertise and commitment in helping to judge the competition entries.

Without the backroom work of Dave Hutton, neither the competition nor this book could have been produced.

Robin Hooppell, Teignmouth, August 2019.

v

Contents

Words Catch Fire
A poem by Jeanna Dobson

There is no such thing as safety words,
Words always catch fire,
You can strike them on stone, on wood,
On the startled faces of strangers.
Write them down to chain them
On paper, on screens, on the back of your hand,
But they fly into the hot wind
Leaving a trail of smoke.
Words can laugh, they can cry,
They can twist the truth,
Words can soothe, can bring joy but
Never forget
They always catch fire.
They leave a singed path that can never
Be extinguished, burnt embers that sear your soul.
Scratching the sky, words become lords,
Sitting amid their own evil beauty.
So toss your words to the four winds,
Catch the ones that others send,
Set free your suffering pen and watch
As the words glow like beacons in the night.

Come Tilly Come
Nicole Fitton

'Come Tilly come.'

I try hard to keep my voice smooth and steady. I am screaming at full volume, but only on the inside. My cheeks are reddening, and I can feel the eyes of those with their perfect dogs burning holes into the back of my head. I will not turn around, I will not. A gentle hand is placed on my shoulder. Chris is by my side; his voice is calm and controlled.

'Take your time Trish, take your time,' he says.

'Call her again.'

He is trying to reassure me. Nothing can reassure me today. Tilly has been perfect all week. She has walked to heel, displaying traits of a well-trained dressage horse. She has looked up at me with her beautiful hazel eyes. Look mum she says, I'm a good girl. You have lulled me into a false sense of security, you cheeky madam. I turned up for Sunday morning training full of hope. I was convinced this would be the week we got to hold our heads high, the week we'd cracked it. I would get to look each one of those self-righteous buggers in the eye and not feel inadequate.

But now, in a field full of farmers, with their perfectly trained gun dogs, the walk of shame is mine, all mine…again. I am setting a new club record for the worst behaved dog ever. You are running at the top of the field without a care in the world, your fluffy spaniel ears flapping away. A straight forward retrieve Chris had said. Nothing straight forward about Tilly I thought. You were perfect, up until the point you were meant to come back. You circled me two, maybe three times, wanting me to be impressed, I wasn't. At least the dummy's still in your mouth, a small consolation I suppose. A live bird would not fare so well

3

with Tilly, I fear. I watch you go and feel envious. You are totally oblivious to my anger and my complete desperation.

Has it really only been three weeks since we commenced this journey through the seventh circle of hell?

'It'll be good for you to get out and meet people, you can't stay cooped up forever,' Mum said in that sage like way only mothers have mastered. Tilly was her idea too.

Daniel has been gone six months and three days. Each day as I wake, the realisation sets in again, and I cry. Great big chunky tears appear from nowhere, and so, the day begins. Tilly knows, somehow, she understands. She lies at the end of my bed, waiting quietly for me to notice her. The days are slightly more bearable now I have a focus, a purpose. Mum was right about so many things I realise.

My days are no longer filled with trips to the hospital, desperately searching for a car parking space close to the Foundation Cancer Unit. The journey was always fractious. I was continuously praying for something – parking space, remission - that sort of thing. I willed each day to be a good day.

Towards the end, I became adept at sussing out where a parking space might be found in that dreadful car park. It had become my thing, my game. It was a way of bringing a line of normality into our fragile, chaotic existence. I would arrive at the unit early, drive once around the block and eye up the possibilities. I spent the best part of two years going around that bloody car park.

If I found a space within 5 minutes, Dan would do well. If it took more than 20 minutes, things would be bad. Those were my rules; after all, it was my game. I even gave it a name – Car Park of Death or CPD for short!

Everyone at the unit was lovely. I didn't want them to be lovely. I wanted them to be harsh and cold and horrid. I wanted to scream and kick and punch.

My first childhood fight had been in infant school with Jade Carter. She'd taken my pencil case and wouldn't give it back. She goaded me, laughing incessantly as I tried to grab it from her. I remember her dark eyes, staring at me, bewildered as I landed a punch square on her jaw line. I wanted the staff at the unit to be like Jade Carter. I wanted a reason to land a punch, to feel the sense of temporary relief I knew it would bring. Instead, I smiled and said 'thank you for everything.'

Finally, the time we craved started to slow. Each day stretched into segments of waiting, regulated only by rounds of drugs and hospital appointments. Was it Tuesday? If it was Tuesday it would be a trip to see the cancer nurse. No, it was Wednesday; Wednesday was chemo day and time to play CPD! Not once did you complain, not once did you cry, but I could see the cracks widening behind your eyes. Like hollow seams within a mine. What little was left was fading fast. I hid my pain, burying it deep beneath a big breath in; you smiled at me and hid yours behind your wobbly teeth.

I tried so hard to dance my words with your feelings, and to begin with, it worked. We found a waltz with the first round of chemo. Smooth and flowing, you sailed through and my words buoyed you.

'Not as bad as I'd expected,' you'd said, your voice hopeful, and I was so damn happy for you, for us. We got pizza and sat by Cathedral Green, and made plans. Big plans -we were now dancing Charleston's. My chatter was upbeat and your smile beamed and nothing could stop us. I brought you a leather jacket.

'On the house,' I'd said and we laughed and you were almost sick with the relief of it all.

'I only married you for the free gifts and chauffeur services,' you said, and you held me tight.

I whispered nonsense into your sweaty neck, and for once I didn't mind the perspiration not one bit. It tasted sweet and balanced out the bitter root of disease.

New words began to silently creep into our vocabulary like stealthy assassins. 'Aggressive' and 'ineffective' disrupted us and stopped us from raising our glitter ball. I put my dancing shoes back into the loft.

'We need to make plans Trish,' you said.

The quiver held at the edge of your voice might as well have been at the end of the universe, because I refused to listen. It's a funny thing hope, and I remained full of it, even as the cliff edge approached.

Our friends no longer visited. Dan was always tired, or his immune system was shot, or both. His eyes had sunken so far back into his head he joked he could now see life from a whole new perspective! His sense of humour; still dark, still deliciously funny. The life we had before his illness was a different life, now only half remembered. I wonder if it were ever real.

It was towards the end of February and bitterly cold when time stood still for Dan and I. Ironically it was not the cancer that got you but a secondary infection – pneumonia.

You wanted to see the snow on the Moors. It had been such a perfect day. We sat in our Mini, wrapped in blankets. Your mum insisted we took those crazy silver space blankets. We had hot water bottles, and thermoses full of tea. I packed your dosette box full of morphine sulphate and multi-coloured pharmaceuticals and off we set.

What a sight we must have been. You were wearing two sweaters, your favourite jeans, two pairs of socks, a thermal jacket, a silly woollen hat with the flappy ears and the crazy space blanket. I couldn't help but smile. You were wrapped

6

up like an expensive Christmas present. You said you knew how a turkey felt and flapped your arms. I could see your pained expression, but I smiled nonetheless. You were but a remnant of the man I had married, but I loved you more than ever that day.

The cold was biting at your bones and I watched you shiver. I felt helpless. You asked me to play Queen's greatest hits. 'Don't stop me now' seemed totally unsuitable as we bumped our way towards Dartmoor, but we hummed along nevertheless. I saw you wince as we encountered a few potholes. I tried my hardest to be more vigilant, scanning the road as best I could. You told me I would lose my PHD if I couldn't pot hole dodge. Even then, you were still the joker, even then I clung to that small seam of you that still shone out.

It was a bright, crisp day. We sat in silence and held hands. Looking out through the windscreen the snow-capped hills looked majestic. Never had they looked so radiant and for that I was grateful. Your breath was shallow and patchy. It was a good way to die. It was your way to die.

As I drove us back 'Another one bites the dust' started to play. Inappropriate? Yes, but your kind of deliciously funny. I knew you were smiling at the absurdity of the situation and that comforted me.

I lived in eternal winter for a while. Numb, lost and wholly unhinged. I didn't feel anything. I would wake up sweating, suffocated I think by sadness, but still I felt nothing.

Only when mum poked her head around the door, that windy April morning, carrying a small bundle of fur with a face, did I feel anything. And so, that was how you came into my life. You didn't know it, but you saved me that day. You, with your helpless energy and undivided loyalty, you saved me. I should have named you naughty dog then, but I fell for your charms and called you Tilly, after a sprightly old lady I once knew. I excused your bad habits, and your odd smells, you were after all a baby and in my care. I needed to look after you.

It's now June. The days are warmer, and the fields are not quite as muddy. The farmers are out in force, ploughing and planting. Eyeing me cautiously, they watch as I'm dragged full pelt through their fields by a flash of liver and white fur. At least you are on your lead at those times. On Sundays however, the farmers of Devon all seem to be standing in the same field as me, radiating an inner smugness. They and their obedient mutts are the crème de la crème. We, young Tilly me girl, we sadly are not. We are what they call a 'work in progress'.

You have ventured closer now but not close enough for me to make a lunge at you. The lesson won't continue until all dogs are under control. All dogs are under control, except for you my crazy darling.

'Call her again,' Chris encourages.

I try to keep the desperation from my voice as I utter my now well-known catch phrase.

'Come Tilly come,' I say trying to make my voice sound light and cheery.

You eye me cautiously. We have been down this road many times during the last few weeks - I do not hold out much hope. But then, as if you know (you always know), you bow your head and slink towards me, dropping the dummy at my feet and sitting up perfectly. I want to kiss you and smack you all at once. Instead I deftly slip the leash around your neck and breathe heavily. I look at you proudly. I have now joined the smug farmers club and it feels good. You look up at me, panting. Your tongue is flopping to one side in a slap stick kind of way and for a moment I am disarmed because you remind me of happier days. We both know who wears the trousers in our house! Dan would have loved you and your stubborn ways.

I start the car and the music shuffles, 'I was born to love you' starts to play and I find myself singing the chorus.

Chris has offered to give us lessons midweek to help bring us (me) up to speed. I can hardly refuse after your Oscar winning performance today. At least I didn't have to jog up the muddy hill like last week, things are definitely looking up.

For all your faults, and believe me I can recite a list the length of your tail, I love you. You listen to my ramblings, to my outbursts of anger at the complete and utter randomness of it all. I know you sense my sadness. The way you lay your head down between your paws and stare up at me. When I feel as if the darkness will never lift, you nuzzle up close, your wet nose warm, reassuring me I'm not alone. I know you understand. You have fed both my heart and my soul.

Tomorrow, I will take you to the beach. Dan loved the beach. I will venture to show you our favourite spots without breaking apart. We'd wander for hours breathing in the salty beauty of the Atlantic. I wonder if you will love it too? I shall tell you about the time we got caught out by the tide and had to make a run for the dunes. How, somewhere along the way the car keys were lost, and how, a rotund man and his metal detector saved the day. You will pad along beside me - yes, you will be on your lead! You will give me a look that says, I'm listening intently and understanding every word, now let me off this darn lead so I can chase whatever takes my fancy… oh look …water … a seagull.

I am thankful for you, my beautiful baby. I may think I am training you, but we both know the truth, don't we my girl?

Closure
Colleen MacMahon

Twelve cruel years had given Jessie Clement plenty of time
to prepare.

Hanging behind the bedroom door were her Sunday Best
black skirt and jacket, not worn since the day of her sister's
funeral, and a brand new white cotton blouse. She had
worried that the blouse was an inappropriate extravagance,
that vanity had governed its purchase rather than propriety.
But truly, whether her picture made it into the newspapers
tomorrow or not, neat attire was surely a mark of respect.
Her most comfortable, low heeled shoes sat beneath the
chair, polished to a chestnut shine in spite of their age, and
the old brown leather purse which almost matched them lay
open and waiting on the dresser. She checked its contents
one last time before snapping it shut.

It was still early but the steaming southern heat was already
making her perspire. The ancient ceiling fan, with its
clattering revolutions, did little more than stir the air and
offer Jessie some company as she readied herself for the
day. The radio stood silent; if there were any more
postponements or last minute appeals Jessie did not intend
to hear about them from some newsman. Not today. They'd
all gorged themselves enough at this feast in her opinion.

Once upon a time Jessie had believed in goodness, she had
trusted that hard work, honesty and common decency
would prevail and that as we sowed, so should we reap. She
had believed all that right up until the minute she had come
back from her annual dental check-up in Atlanta to find her
sister dead on the porch. It had taken her a full minute to
understand what she was seeing, to recognise the twisted,
bloodied, half naked grotesque as her beloved Ellie-May and
to take in what had happened. At first she looked upwards
and around her for some explanation – had the sky fallen in

11

or some terrible thunderbolt struck the house and killed her sister? Even when she saw the bloody kitchen knife lying by Ellie- May's side she did not fully comprehend. In the Clement sisters' world people did not do this to each other.

Twelve years had taught Jessie an awful lot. They had taught her that violent young men got high on drink and drugs and raped and murdered innocent women. They had taught her about things like forensics and DNA, about police methods, capture, court procedures and conviction. She had learned more than she could ever have imagined about cruelty.

Frankie Bridger was apprehended within twenty four hours of Ellie-May's last painful breath. He was tried and sentenced within a twelve month of that. More than a decade later Jessie Clement was going to witness him paying for his crime and would finally have what the press labelled 'closure' and her minister called 'peace'.

After a second shower Jessie took particular care with deodorant and cologne and put on her blouse. It buttoned up high and therefore respectable, she thought as she surveyed herself in the big mahogany mirror. There was no getting away from the fact that the skirt and jacket were too big for her now; Jessie had always been lean but years of grief and stress had stripped her further. Nevertheless, with her hair scraped back into a bun and a sombre black felt beret on her head she looked neat and tidy which was what mattered.

She left the house at eight a.m. precisely. She could see Tyrone striding up the dustpath towards her and she kept her voice steady and normal as he reached the porch,

"'Mornin' Tyrone. Thank you for being so punctual, I surely appreciate it."

"Oh, that's okay, ma'am. I know how important today is and I…well, I wish you well."

"Thank you, Tyrone. Now, I loaded up the pumpkins on the cart last night but y'all feel free to add more if you think there's ripe ones I missed. Don't park too close to the highway – I don't want you coming to mischief on my account – but make sure folks can see you and the sign with all the prices on. Here's the cash box with plenty of change and I left an ice box on the porch there with cold drinks and some lunch for you. I'll be back late this afternoon I would imagine."

"Don't worry, Miss Clement, I'll just stay here till you get back or I run out of pumpkins – whichever comes first." He wanted to say more, to tell her that he felt sorry for her, that he wished there was more he could do to help, that she was a kind and gentle person who did not deserve all the sorrow and meanness she had suffered in her life. Tyrone had not known the two sisters at the time of Ellie-May's murder, being only five at the time, but their story was woven into the tapestry of local history. He knew Jessie had looked after her deaf mute sister since they were young, neither had married and they had simply lived for each other.

Nonetheless, as he stepped onto the porch to collect the ice box, the place had no macabre associations for him as it had for Jessie. He had not seen the deck awash with blood, the torn clothing scattered and flapping in the breeze, the door screen swinging and creaking behind the tableau as if opening and closing its mouth in a series of screams.

Jessie's life was all about memories, she struggled constantly to escape them. It was why the radio was always on, why she toiled on the little homestead way past exhaustion and why, when she wasn't working, she read until her mind was numb. Once, she had bought a small television set cheaply from a neighbour thinking that it might distract her but she was sickened by what she saw. The language, the violence and the apparent glorification of depravity were not what she considered entertaining. She had given the television to

Tyrone.

A horn blasted in the distance and Jessie checked her watch. She said her farewells to Tyrone and set off down the path, aware of his sympathetic eyes watching her back as she passed like a mirage through the sticky heat and arrived at the scrubby verge of the highway just seconds before the bus. Strictly speaking the stop was a quarter of a mile down the road at the Piggly Wiggly store but Chester always hooted the horn ahead, giving Jessie time just to walk down from the house if she wanted to catch his bus into town. This was the kind of world the Clement sisters had grown up in, a place where folk looked out for their neighbors and were not shy to offer or accept help. As she boarded the bus, nodding a greeting to Chester because she felt she could not trust her voice, she felt the wave of love and support as she moved down the aisle, people gently touching her arms or squeezing her hands as she passed.

It was an ordeal, meant kindly but something she had been dreading almost more than any other part of the day because she had known it would make her cry. Once she was safely seated at the back she took a little cotton hankie from her purse and dabbed at her eyes. The bus rumbled off and she concentrated hard on the passing landscape, her stomach knotted with anxiety and hunger. She'd been unable to face breakfast. When she got home the table would still be set for that first meal of the day; napkin carefully folded next to the bowl, the plate and the cutlery and the pans ready on the stove for grits and hash browns. The light would most probably be fading by then, Tyrone would have brought the cart back to the barn and loaded it up ready for the next day and Jessie would switch the radio on, once again able to listen to the news. Unless. Unless something had gone wrong and there had been yet another delay, a successful appeal, a last minute act of clemency…

The gentle, good natured Jessie of twelve years ago would

not have believed that she could want anyone to die but her feelings about Frankie Bridger plumbed depths of loathing and abhorrence she could not have imagined. She would never get her sister back but she wanted to close the curtains tonight on a day which had brought retribution and justice at least.

There were no extenuating circumstances as far as Jessie was concerned, no possible excuses for that monster's actions when he randomly chose their pathway to walk up and violate her sister. Ellie would not have heard him coming. She would have been quietly going about her day cleaning, baking and gardening when the tall, foul smelling figure suddenly appeared beside her, grinning with delight at the unexpected gift before him. Later, while he left her dying on the porch, he helped himself to milk and meat from the refrigerator which he regurgitated in the kitchen. Then he defecated in the hallway and the parlour before walking past her, through the blood, to sleep off his exertions in a nearby field.

Frankie Bridger had not come from a bad environment; he had a reasonably happy, loving upbringing in a home no poorer or more deprived than most. He had not suffered abuse, or neglect, or lack of opportunities to make something of his life. He just went bad all by himself. It was hard for anyone to find anything convincing to say in his defence. He had committed an horrific crime and most everyone agreed with Jessie – he deserved to die.

At a quarter after nine Jessie boarded a second bus. She left her little home town to travel amongst strangers and was glad of it. Now she could sit anonymously and use this last hour to gather her thoughts and courage. She knew that what lay ahead would not be easy; she did not relish the prospect of watching an execution, wanting only to be done with waiting for Frankie Bridger to depart the world. She had no doubt he would burn in Hell but that was The

Lord's responsibility, not hers. She would have done her duty by her sister and seen things through to the bitter end.

The rising heat and failing air-con turned the bus into a sweltering box; people were fanning themselves with anything that came to hand – newspapers, straw hats, pocket diaries. All Jessie had was an envelope containing directions, information and scheduling for the day and she would rather melt than show disrespect by using that. She folded her jacket on her lap, loosened the top buttons of her blouse and rested her head against the window. Her forehead and upper lip were clammy and the knots in her stomach had hardened into concrete. It was all she could do to rise and stagger to the front of the bus as her stop approached. She stepped down onto the sidewalk and stood for a moment, dizzy and nauseous but determined not to faint. Just yards away, milling around the entrance to the Death House yard, was the expected crowd of press, protestors and bystanders and the last thing Jessie wanted was to draw attention to herself.

Across the road was a paved area with a drinking fountain and an old metal bench. Jessie crossed over and bent down to take a long cool drink, then she soaked the little cotton handkerchief in water and patted at her face. The bench was painfully hot and the slats beneath her bottom were uncomfortable but afforded her the chance to sit for a while, watching the scene in front of her whilst she composed herself.

Half a dozen people were marching up and down with placards, chanting slogans and calling for the condemned man's release. Shouting them down was a mob of Pro Death supporters, some of them screaming and gesticulating so violently Jessie was alarmed.

She watched the activity across over the road with an increasing sense of unreality. Aside from the chorus of demonstrators it seemed as if everyone else could just as easily have been queuing outside Starbucks for a coffee; the reporters stood around chatting, chewing gum and hassling the cops for an early entry into the yard. The police, for their part, were sombre and professional but otherwise indistinct from their counterparts directing traffic down the road. Inside that dreadful building, thought Jessie, was a man about to face his last moments on this earth. He had woken (if indeed he had been able to sleep) to his final dawn and eaten (had he been able to raise the appetite) his ultimate meal. It occurred to her that, sickened and upset as she felt, she could not come close to imagining his fear. What must he be feeling as he waited to walk into a room he knew he would never leave and enter a purgatory he could never escape?

Time was marching on. The gates were opened and people, after careful vetting of papers and passes, were allowed in. A young woman, pale and uneasy in an uncomfortably heavyweight business suit, had joined the group of reporters; they were searched and ushered towards the main entrance where they were questioned and searched once again. Then they disappeared into the mouth of the building.

Jessie swallowed hard to quell another wave of nausea. Then she rose, buttoned the collar of her blouse and smoothed her skirt. It was time to go.

The next morning, as he sat by the cart with its fresh load of pumpkins, Tyrone opened the newspaper. The front page headlines contained the bald statement of Frankie Bridger's death and a warning of imminent bad weather on the East coast. In the bottom corner was a coupon for discount car tyres which he must remember to cut out for his mom. He turned to the third page, shifting the paper to better position it in shade.

DENTON COUNTY TRIBUNE   October 16th 2012

SADISTIC KILLER FRANKIE BRIDGER FINALLY EXECUTED

By Melissa Tyler-Brookes

"Yesterday I witnessed my first execution, not an experience I ever wish to repeat but one which I'm obliged to share. Whilst the debate over our continued implementation of the death penalty in this state rumbles on I'd like you to know some details which might help to inform your opinion on the subject.

In case you need reminding of the events of twelve years ago which led to Frankie Bridger's death by lethal injection yesterday, here are the bare facts: After a two day binge on alcohol and drugs a twenty nine year old white male stumbled upon a lone, forty seven year old, deaf-mute woman (also white – there was no racist motive) in her home on the outskirts of the sleepy town of Shersville. He raped, tortured and slaughtered Ellie-May before defiling the inside of the house she shared with her fifty three year old sister who was, most unusually, out for the entire day. When Jessica Clement returned she discovered her sister's mutilated body on the porch.

Bridger was found asleep in a nearby field within hours. He was arrested and tried and pleaded guilty to all charges. He was sentenced to death by lethal injection and has been incarcerated in Death Row ever since. The date set for the execution has been postponed four times following appeals, demands for re-trials (on the unfounded basis of new evidence being forthcoming) and the instatement of a new Governor - Edward Percival III - subsequent to the demise of Gene Warburton. However, it transpired that Governor Percival is as strong an advocate of capital punishment as his predecessor.

Denton County Death House is a squat, white building which might appear nondescript and unthreatening were it not for its associations, but there is no escaping a macabre atmosphere once inside. Separated from the actual execution chamber by a glass window is the spectator room where there are three rows of chairs. The back row is reserved for the media and yesterday it was fully occupied by local and national press. Immediately in front of us were the Defence attorneys – till the last possible moment still discussing the possibility of a "Stay" – and court officials. The front row is always reserved for the families of the condemned and his victim(s) and on this occasion only one of those chairs was occupied.

When everyone was seated a clerk gave us all a quick, matter of fact briefing. We were informed that seated in the front row was Frankie's father Jackson Bridger - his mother Susan being too ill to attend. Jessica Clement, the victim's sister, had apparently waived her right to be present at the very last minute. There was a mixed response to this announcement; some were shocked, since Jessica had been known to attend every possible event – from trial through to hearings, debates and demonstrations – in connection with her sister's murder, every one of which must have been harrowing and upsetting. From my perspective, and with my admittedly limited knowledge of the lady, this came as no surprise however. She has always struck me as a shy and gentle soul – much as her sister was, according to those who knew her. In spite of her obvious commitment to Ellie-May's memory and her determination to see justice done, Jessica has eschewed the limelight as much as possible and declined to be interviewed in any formal sense. She has not relished the attention or exploited it as some might have done. I cannot be sure of this but I suspect she simply could not face this final brutal act.

It was not my intention in this article to do other than report and inform, leaving you to draw your own conclusions about the continued viability of capital punishment in a morally evolved society, so I shall continue with the facts.

At twelve minutes after eleven the condemned man was escorted into the chamber by five guards and strapped onto the gurney by each foot, knee and arm, with a final single strap across his torso. Two women (who, like all the prison staff involved, were volunteers) then attached heart monitoring equipment to his chest, put syringes in both arms and connected these to intravenous drips. One of the guards placed surgical tape around Bridger's fingertips, securing them to the gurney which was then raised to an upright angle facing the viewing room. It seemed to me that his eyes searched the spectators' gallery for someone in particular before settling on his father's face; one can only imagine what that poor man must have felt as he exchanged this very last look with his son.

Every one of us observing the minutiae of the ritual before us was conscious of the seconds ticking by and the two telephones sitting at the side of the chamber. The red phone is connected to Governor Percival's office in case of an eleventh hour reprieve and the white phone goes through to the Prison Warden's office should news of a stay of execution come through by fax.

The warden cleared his throat and made a formal announcement through the microphone:

"We are here for the execution of Franklyn Dwight Bridger with all witnesses present. I would ask you all to remain silent." Then, turning to the man lying on the gurney, "Do you, Franklyn Dwight Bridger, have anything to say?"

There was no dramatic pause, no apparent epiphany for Frankie as he immediately shook his head and grinned at his father. It was a horrible moment, impossible to interpret as anything but mockery, and at this Jackson Bridger dropped his head into his hands and began to weep. He did not raise his head again.

The warden read the death warrant and the process began. First the pentobarbital, a sedative which had no discernible effect since Bridger seemed extraordinarily calm already. Then pancuronium bromide which, according to whom you believe, is either an humane muscle relaxant or a paralytic designed not to spare the recipient pain but to spare the audience observing his suffering. Yesterday we were spared nothing. Bridger began to grimace and gasp for air as, technically, he was starting to suffocate. With the administration of the final drug, potassium chloride, Bridger struggled for several minutes before succumbing to full cardiac arrest.

At this point two doctors checked his eyes and his pulse and held stethoscopes to his chest. They both nodded and the warden cleared his throat again, "At eleven forty six a.m., October fifteenth two thousand and twelve, the court-ordered execution of Franklyn Dwight Bridger was carried out in accordance with the laws of Georgia."

Then the curtains were drawn between us and the chamber, and it was over.

Ellie-May Clement, by the best forensic estimates, died approximately two hours after Frankie first clamped his hand (quite unnecessarily had he but known it) over her mouth. Frankie Bridger took sixteen minutes to expire."

Tyrone read the article twice then slipped the newspaper quickly under his stool as he saw Jessie Clement coming down the path. She carried a tray with a cloth and cutlery all neatly laid, a glass of ice cold lemonade and the biggest po'boy sandwich Tyrone had ever seen, stuffed with succulent cold meats and salads and oozing mayo. There was a thick paper napkin cupping two fine apples for dessert.

"Here y'all go, Tyrone, I expect you're about ready for this."

"I sure am, Miss Clement, but you didn't need to go to so much trouble."

"No trouble at all, Tyrone. I'm feeling very much better today."

"I'm very relieved to hear that, ma'am."

When she had stepped off the bus the previous afternoon, several hours earlier than expected, Tyrone had felt obliged to assist her all the way up to the house in spite of her protests. He wanted to call a doctor but Jessie said no, she would be just fine after a good night's sleep if Tyrone didn't mind closing up at the end of the day and setting up again in the morning. He said he would be happy to, poured her some iced tea and went back to the pumpkins. Sales were good, what with Hallowe'en coming up and all and he wanted the stall to do well for her sake.

Now she was smiling and looking stronger than she had for many months. A sudden breeze picked up a corner of the newspaper, nudging it out from under the stool and Tyrone moved to kick it out of sight.

"It's alright, Tyrone, I've already seen it. No harm done." She looked so genuinely serene and relaxed that the boy felt able to say, "If you don't mind me asking, ma'am, why didn't you go yesterday? You seemed all set to when you left here."

"Yes, I was. I got all the way to the place and just couldn't do it. Couldn't watch a man die in cold blood, no matter what he'd done. In fact, if I'd thought it would hold any sway at all I'd have called the Governor and asked him to stop it. Oh, don't look at me as if I'm some kind of saint, Tyrone – I'm not so good a person. I don't forgive that man his terrible wickedness but watching him die was never going to be the right way to honor my sister. She wouldn't have done it if things had been the other way around. She'd have buried me and mourned me and waited to join me one

22

day when her time came, but she wouldn't have wasted her precious life here on God's earth in the meantime frettin' about revenge. Now look lively, young feller, there's a car coming down the road and I'm just betting that's some folk wanting to buy a whole heap of pumpkins."

How Do I Feel About Lentils?
Anna Barker

The boy's in the hide. Seen him a couple of times now with his camera. Nice lad. I try to summon his name. It's there, at the edges. Reminds me of Phillip at that age, lanky, feet a bit too big for him, like a Moorhen chick. He'll grow into them. What's his name? No, won't come. Should've written it down.

'All right,' he says.

'Now then. How's it looking?'

'You just missed an Avocet.'

'Never. You get a photo?'

'Yeah, but it's not great.'

I peer over his shoulder while he searches for it in his camera. Got a good eye, great shot of a Sandpiper. 'That's a belter, that one.'

'Yeah, got lucky. I was up near Emmanuel Point, you know where it shelves down and then there's a drop?'

I try to think where he means, but nothing comes. 'Aye, I know it.'

He finds the Avocet. 'I didn't get the eye in focus.'

'No, get the eye and you've got the shot, doesn't matter if the feathers are a bit out, as long as you get the eye.'

He nods. Maybe I told him that before. I set up further along the bench. The window's up and stiff. I try to lower it, but it gets stuck half-way. He sees me struggling and comes over, easily turning the knob the rest of the way around.

'I could hardly get mine down either,' he says.

I suspect it isn't true. Nice lad. His nails are bitten to the quick, dirt ground into the cuticles. Phillip planting tulip bulbs in the tub on the patio. I see us there, side-by-side, me kneeling on a cushion. I'm handing him the bulbs, telling him how deep to make the hole. Years ago. Before we fell out, though what we fell out about I don't know. I did, once. Must've. I try to recall my last conversation with him, but it's just an image, his face full of anger, no words.

'Thank you, Phillip.'

'Toby.'

'Ah, yes, so it is.'

He gives me a shy sideways smile and returns to his spot on the bench.

'You enjoying your holiday then?'

He shrugs. 'Yeah, I guess. Told me mates I was going to New York.'

'I went to Montana once, had an uncle lived there. New York, eh?'

'If they knew I was going birding they wouldn't half take the piss.'

He looks through his camera, focuses on something I can't see, takes a shot.

'Tell 'em you've seen a Pallus warbler, that'll shut them up.'

'A what…?'

'Two sightings in forty years. That's in the whole of the UK, mind.'

A smile, shakes his head.

For a minute or two we look out over the pond, a silence settling between us. Been birding on my own for so long I've forgotten what it's like to have company, though this lad's quieter than Tommy. By heck, Tommy, we had some crack. Not thought of him for years. Killed in action on that bloody beach, first day, was it? Or was it the second? He'd have been what, nineteen. Not that much older than this lad.

He's spotted something. A grebe? Haven't got my binoculars out yet. 'So why would they take the piss then?'

He puts down his camera. Maybe I'm a bother, but then he says: 'Birding just isn't cool. I mean, for someone my age. Ok, if you're…'

'Old?'

He rubs his nose.

'Oh, don't worry yourself, lad. I'm eighty-three,

that's plenty old. Here,' I offer him one of the pasties Mary fetched from the bakers. 'Get your mits round that.'

'Thanks.'

'Me and this mate of mine, Tommy Pigeon, we'd go out every weekend birding when we were your age. We had a book, bit like you've got there.'

'He wasn't called Tommy Pigeon though, was he?'

'He wasn't? I don't know, you might be right.'

'No, I mean, pigeon.'

'Oh I see.' Yes, I remember now, it was a thing him having a name like that. 'No, definitely Pigeon. Girls loved him, real charmer. Wasn't for Tommy I wouldn't have met Mary.'

'How come?'

'There was this girl Tommy fancied, Kathy or Kate, something like that, anyway he gets her and her friend, Mary, to come birding with us.'

'What, like a date?'

'Suppose it was. First date. You got a girl?'

'Be serious.' He looks away, flicks bits of pastry off his jeans.

'Why not? Nowt wrong with you.' Shy, mind. Suppose I was no different. 'Well, you want a girl, you take her birding.'

'Not the lasses at my school, they'd sooner stick pins in their eyes.'

'Best place for a date, a hide.'

'Yeah?'

'Oh go on, use your imagination.'

'Ah what, did you just wink?' He laughs then, proper belly laugh. 'You're glass, man, pure glass.'

Class, I think he says, sounded like glass, but I'm not sure what being glass would be about. Talk funny kids these days, but then there was that thing Phillip used to say…Square, that's right. Everything was square.

'You been married a long time then, you and…Mary?'

'Sixty-one years, or it could be sixty-four. She'd tell you.'

He sucks in a breath. 'That's ages.'

'Yep.'

'Won't she be mad at you not remembering?'

'Got a get out of jail free card.' I tap the side of my head. 'Don't remember stuff like I used to.'

'You remembered Tommy Pigeon.'

'So I did.' Funny, I don't often tell people about me forgetting things, but somehow I don't mind telling this kid. Maybe it's easier to be old around the young. 'I got a trick up my sleeve though, see?' I open my logbook at random. 'I write stuff down, used to just be a record of birds, but now…what does that say…?'

He slides over, tries to read my handwriting. 'Time, and

28

date, I think.'

'No, not there, this extra column.' I slip my specs on, read from the top. 'There, you see? Mary's birthday. Warfarin clinic, 2.15. Put the bins out. It's like a trail of breadcrumbs I lay for myself.'

He points to an entry on the opposite page. 'An Eastern Black Redstart? Always wanted to see one of them.'

'Ah yes, now when was that?'

'You've written it down, look, May 11th, 2002.'

'Drove two hundred miles for that fella, I did.' I laugh, startled at my memory of it, clear as the day I wrote it down. 'Wouldn't think twice about driving two hundred miles then, mad, though, isn't it, when you come to think of it? Just on the off chance you might get a glimpse.'

'I dunno, I think it's pretty cool. You got one you're still after?'

I close the book. 'Aye, maybe.'

'Can I guess?'

'Go on then.'

'Osprey?'

'Bigger.'

'What's bigger?' He looks confused. 'Golden Eagle?'

'A migration.'

'Yeah, but that's not one bird.'

'No, thousands, not all at once, of course, but there's usually one night when there's so many of them they almost fill the sky. Here, Sandham Cove?'

He nods.

'Or at least I suppose they do. Donkey's years I've been

coming here and I still haven't seen it.'

'But doesn't it happen every year?'

'Aye, but when, which night?' A memory of Tommy hunkered down in the shadow of a dune. 'I suppose you might say it's my holy grail. You'll have yours, too, I expect.'

He looks out over the pond. 'I just like taking pictures.'

'You better get some more then.'

He shuffles back over to his spot, but we don't chat much after that until he's ready to move on to his next pitch. 'Might have a look round Sandham Cove,' he says. Then he's off. I watch him from the hide window, waving when he looks back, then I follow his path across the open fields on to the reserve until he's out of sight.

I hang around a bit, but I don't settle. The hide has a different quality, changed by his presence, emptier now he's gone. I look out, just a few ducks anyhow. They're a jittery lot, a change of mood sees them bluster across the water, rise as one with a great clack and then skid into the reed stalks. Maybe a fox about. I pack up, feeling tired, the walk back suddenly a chore.

Outside it's got colder, the fields gripped by frost. Better get a move on, Mary'll be getting worried. I check my hand-clock. Funny slip, that one. I said it to her last week, the word 'watch' just wouldn't come. We laughed about it. Now, of course, we call it a hand-clock all the time. At least we can still laugh. I tug my hat down over my ears and put my head into the wind. It's a challenge to walk in it, gusts from every which way, but mostly it blows straight off the sea and I have to pit my weight against it. I push on, just the occasional stagger now and then.

Tide's out I see, oystercatchers have gathered on the ribbed sand in their usual state of constant vigilance, hair trigger responses to dangers unseen, but felt. I think of Tommy, always young, of Phillip, always angry, but their faces are a blur like I'm looking at them through mist.

Mary doesn't get angry - as well she might - but I hear the note of strained patience in her voice sometimes. We're not going to let it spoil things, she says. But there's stuff I don't tell her about, how once, or maybe twice, I've woken in the night, seen her beside me and not known her. It'd hurt her, that. Such nonsense anyway. Like coming to out of a dream, that's all it is, seconds only, gone the moment I curl into her back, get her smell.

As I reach the familiar line of grave oak trees I look up to their branches. Last year's dry leaves are shivering out notes. Funny, I see those leaves and immediately I think 'oak', and yet I couldn't get 'watch.'

I look around me, fixing on all the other things I can name as well today as I could yesterday: tight buds on the hawthorn, nipped-looking crocuses dotting the grass verge, a scab of yellow-crusted lichen on the wall.

That's the trick, Mary says. As long as I don't stray from what's familiar I can choose a single moment and be right in it, my mind will stay there with me. I can keep it whole.

We eat early in the restaurant; dusk falling on the garden. The boy's at a table with his parents, he gives me a timid nod as I pass, but I don't stop, don't want to embarrass the lad. Mary chooses a spot by the window. I see a mistle thrush high on a branch in the apple tree, feathers ruffled by the wind, singing his heart out the way they do when there's a storm coming. Storm-cock. Aye, that's his other name.

'Are you hungry?' Mary says.

'Eat a horse.'

'Didn't you have your pasties?'

'Gave one to the lad.' I nod in his direction. He's on his

phone, his parents deep in conversation. 'Saw him in the hide.'

I want to ask her why Phillip's angry, but I know it'll upset her and she's made a bit of an effort, got her nice necklace on and her blue dress. It'll come to me. I put my specs on to look at the menu, but it's the same as last night. Cottage pie, sea bass. Lentil curry.

'How do I feel about lentils?' I ask her.

'You like them.'

Play havoc with me insides, mind, but I need something to perk me up or I'll be nodding off before Mary gets her pudding. As it is she skips it and we move into the bar, Mary with her half lager and me with my Guinness. We're playing pontoon for pennies when the boy and his parents come out of the dining room. I see them dither in the foyer a while, deciding what to do, then they leave and cross the car park into the village.

'Pontoon,' Mary says.

'Again?'

She sets her cards down on the table.

'Ah well, I'm done in anyhow. Think I'll go up to bed.'

A fist of wind thumps the glass. Must be what woke me. Yes, there it is again. Takes a minute for my eyes to adjust then I locate the window, only it's in the wrong place. I turn over in bed; jerk my head back. A woman, no idea who she is. Bloody hell. There'll be ructions, I'll have to – no, hang on, wait a minute. It's Mary.

Best not wake her. I look for my hand-clock, see it on the bedside table beside me. My eye things are there too, so I needn't clatter about, just get some clothes on and then I'll be on my way. Be at Sandham Cove before sunrise.

I creep downstairs and out into the car park. Lamps are still burning. Cold morning for it. I check my wrist, but the hand-clock's not there, didn't pick it up. No matter. One of the other lads'll have a clock. Barry Pigeon. I'll have a look in on him when I get there. He'll have marked out his spot already.

Tommy.

Mary's voice. I look around for her, but she's not here. That'll just be her in my head then. I hear her sometimes, putting me right.

His name's Tommy Pigeon.

Can't be, I tell her, what sort of a name's that? She'll be right, though, no doubt.

'Come on, Tommy,' I say. 'I'll carry your eye things, you take the sack.'

No answer. He must've gone on ahead. Keen as muck he is. That's right, I remember now, told him I'd say bye to Mary then catch him up. I expect she's gone to pick the kids up. Got to get going anyway, don't want to miss it. I look at the sky, the shell of the moon, no bombers though. By God, that wind, nearly blows you off your feet.

I cross the road, see the castle ahead. Should've put my big coat on 'cos there's snow now too, just a few flakes, trying their luck. I go through a gate, get into the shelter of a hedge. Almost forgot the way for a second, but no, this is right, I remember now. Sometimes I forget things, Mary'll tell you. That's it, here's the bridge with the stream that's always gargling under it. Tough going in this wind, mind. I have to lean into it, put me head down to meet each blast. Not far now. Tommy'll have a brew on in his tent I expect, warm us up. Yes, you see that fence post with the large stone beside it? There, just on the other side of that it's the dunes.

The path's thinning.

SINGLE FILE, MEN, HEADS DOWN!

The wind's blowing straight off the sea, breaks my stride a couple of times then a big gust punches me and I fall against the wall.

HOLD THE LINE THERE! HOLD THE LINE!

I find my feet again, straighten up, march on. My ear's stinging, but I pay it no mind and before long I reach the path that squirrels into the dunes. A bush snags me as I pass, tearing a hole in my fleece.

I told you to take your big coat, soaked through, you daft ha'peth.

'Ah, Mary, there you are. It's tonight. I'm finally going to see it.'

See what, love?

I look up at the sky. 'Planes, three, no, five! It's all right, they're ours.'

They're past me in a flash. Climb a dune, get a proper look from there, but the grass is a real pain, keeps getting wound round me feet. One more dune then it's the beach.

Careful. You fall at your age, you break something.

I'm all right, don't be fussing. By Hell, it's all up and down though, takes the puff out of me. Tommy'll be laughing his head off. Does a mile in under five minutes, Tommy, makes dust of the lot of us. Aye well, I'm coming, you bugger. I half-run, half-slide to the bottom of the dune and then look around.

You should come back now, love, get warm.

All right, all right. Chattering on, can't a man think? Which way? There's the path now, something lying on it. Looks like a rock, but it's not a rock. It's a bird, shot down. Your mates have left you, I tell him, no choice, that's how it is

34

sometimes.

'Tommy!'

He'll have some tea, Tommy will, p'raps even something a bit stronger to keep the cold out. My teeth are clattering. Just along this way, got to be. All I have to do is stay inside the moment then I can keep it whole.

This way, you silly sod.

She's right. Always knows what to do, Mary.

I hear the sea before I see it; angry as hell, but then I cross the beach and there's nothing in front of me except waves, rising, falling, hurling themselves against the cliffs. The spray stings my eyes.

Can't see Tommy. No one else from my unit either, but I'm sure they said here. Got me wires crossed probably. I see a tooth of rock jutting out of the sand: a monster, might be the head of a dragon, or just a dressing gown on the back of the door. Not real.

Go back to sleep, love. Just a dream.

Something's trickling down my neck. My hand finds a cut on my ear, wet with blood, but I don't remember how it got like that. The wind comes at me again, another whack, but I know I'm no match for it so I just sit down on the sand.

That's right, love, get your breath back.

I've forgotten where she is. Not here. Well, thank God she's not, it's not safe. I'll just lay low 'til Tommy comes. I think I can hear him, his voice calling, but I can't work out what he's saying. Too far away. Several voices now, there must be somebody with him.

I crane my neck. Radio calls, are they? Yes, that's it. Just the one plane at first, then I see others dropping down through a thick stretch of cloud. Dark shapes, a whole row of V's, at least three squadrons. Another group to my right, even bigger, too many to count. Our boys, our boys coming home.

I stagger to my feet, snatching at my eye things, but they're twisted, can't get them up to my face in time. Where you at, man, you're missing it. No greater sight than a Spitfire squadron, Tommy. That'll put the fear of God into 'em. Listen to that roar.

Another gust, I'm not braced, it drops me to my knees. I haul myself up just in time to see two fall from the sky, spiralling, like they're made of nothing, scraps of paper. They crash on the beach a hundred yards ahead, but before I can reach them another comes straight at me, losing height. It swerves to my right, heads out to sea, and then hits the water with a smack.

There's hundreds, Tommy, almost fill the sky, but they shouldn't be trying to land in this storm. They don't stand a chance.

I stagger forward, trying to reach the wreckage of one that's just come down, only it isn't there anymore. I turn, scan the beach, gone, just a feathery thing there now, a what's-it, a bird, aye, that's it, lying on his back, poor thing. I reach out to right it, but it struggles, beats its wings, then he slips sidewards, all the fight gone from him. Another there. This one's hit the deck so hard his head's come clean away. They're everywhere now, dead or dying.

A churring of wings makes me look up again. It's the biggest group yet, but no sooner have they dipped below the clouds than the rank breaks. Some ditch into the dunes, others find shelter in a crevice on the cliff, safe, but only for a minute. I watch as the waves pick them off and one after the other they fall into the sea. So many. I wander among them, gazing at their broken bodies, wings torn, necks twisted, eyes glazed and staring at the sky.

A light further along the beach, swinging left and right, an odd dance, then I see him, just his outline at first. Tommy, at last. He's running toward me.

'You're bleeding,' he says, skidding to a halt.

'There you are.'

He's taking off his coat. He wraps it around my shoulders. I feel its warmth.

'Everybody's out looking for you.'

'I got separated.'

I point to the bodies lying around us, but he's not got the stomach for it, he's still busying himself with the coat, trying to do up the whizzer, but his fingers are too cold.

'The others all went to the causeway,' he says. 'They thought you'd try to get across to the mainland. But then I remembered what you said in the hide.'

No wonder then. There's been a right cock up. They're not supposed to be at the causeway, they're meant to be here. He's scrabbling inside the pocket of the coat, gets this thing out, what it's called? Lights up. He's jabbing at the thing. Phone. That's it.

Daft beggar, he's not Tommy. He's the Moorhen chick. Tommy was here a minute ago though, wasn't he? Where's he gone? I look for him, but there's just the boy.

Sandham Cove he keeps saying.

'They're coming. Think you can make it into the dunes? It'll be more sheltered there.'

I nod. Likes taking pictures. Thinks I'm glass. Nice lad. I reach for his hand, but he takes my wrist instead, a roman handshake. We have to step around the birds. The white belly of the plover, the red throat of the swallow, the black neckerchief of the little ringed plover.

'Lot's made it,' he says.

I look at him.

'No, really, I saw them. Bound to lose a few, right?'

'Aye.'

'C'mon, Mary'll be worried.'

Mary. I picture her now. She's in her blue dress, looking at me across a table.

'You don't want to worry her.'

No, I don't want to worry her. Back home to Mary. I'll tell her about Tommy and the crash landings and how I got separated. She'll know what to do.

Rebuffed
Michael J Fleming

Phase One

Fun, good sex, joke-sharing, creative co-energy, encouragement, large thin-based pepperoni pizzas with extra mushrooms washed down with cold Amstels, company when company was needed and space when it wasn't – those were the things we craved. We were traders of malleable thoughts. You scatting free verse, all angst and anger; me engineering sonnets and little acid pieces that you said were tantamount to Larkin about. Then you broke through with The Net-Caster. You told me you wouldn't have submitted it to Poetry Review without my encouragement. I felt an envy-free pride at the time. I'm still proud – it's a scintillating poem. It hangs over my battered desk. I'm looking at it now as I listen to the tattoo of warm rain on the window.

The Net-Caster was the first success either of us had had. And I felt good for you. I called my dad and told him you'd been published. At that time, you two had yet to meet. Your success seemed to be the opportunity for him to badger me into taking you to Thorpeness.

*

This is my dad, Chris, I say. Dad, this is Emily. You hold out your hand but he ignores that and gives you a peck on the cheek and a hug. Blimey, steady on Dad, I think but don't say. I can see your body stiffen. I should have warned him that you're not the tactile type when dressed. I should have warned you that Chris's awareness of feminism is rough-hewn. When he pulls your dining chair out, I wince. You play it with a serenity that impresses me. You're cutting Chris some slack; extending a line of credit on an unassessed risk.

Chris keeps pouring the red and asking you, and for balance me, about the writing process: subject-matter; choice of metre and, alarmingly, rhyming-scheme. He seems genuinely surprised, shocked even, that you've never written anything traditional unless it was to order. He clears his throat and announces that his rhyming-schemes of choice are A, B, A, B and A, A, B, B. He misinterprets the look of astonishment on my face, holds up a confessional finger and says, that to be hair-splittingly correct, he has written a handful of poems in A, B, B, A. Noticing that I'm still open-mouthed he confirms that he has recently taken up, as he puts it, the quill. He points to the three piles of paper on the sideboard. He says he can read us a few, if we'd care to hear them.

Working to keep any hint of panic from my voice I suggest we leave it until the morning, when we're all fresh. I'm thinking that by then I'll have come up with some engagement that screams for our attendance elsewhere. You read me like a Ladybird Book and say you'd love to hear some of Chris's (and you pause here and give me the merest hint of a sidelong glance) musings. You stretch out and plant your stripy-socked feet on the fourth chair - the one Mum used to occupy when it was the second chair and she and the dining-room set were in Chiswick together with Chris and, on occasion, me. Chris doesn't seem to mind as he carries the first of his piles to the table. He tops up the glasses.

Face flushed, he tells us these are poems based on homophones. I think this one will crack you up, he says, seeking to manage its reception. It's called, Threw a Glass Darkly.

I threw a glass darkly,

In a terrible mood,

It bounced off the table,

And scattered the food,

40

It clattered the window,

And shattered the pane,

Throw a glass darkly?

Never again.

I manage an appreciative nod, shifting in my chair. You clap your hands and call out for another. You're playing the perfect guest. Chris is puffed up like a feather pillow. He flicks through the sheaf and, with a lick of the thumb, selects another page. This one, he announces, is a young boy talking to his mother. I'm not saying it's biographical, he announces with a smile presented as playful but which I can only read as wistful. It's called Three Point One Four.

"That peach pie's way too small no doubt,"

I said to Mum with some concern.

"Of course it's not, I've worked it out,

It's something you should learn.

Taking the pastry and the peach,

And given it's equally shared,

That's three point one four slices each:

Cooks call that pi r squared."

You throw your head back and roar. I'm bewildered.

After another eight of Chris's poems I suggest to you we hit the sack. You say you'll join me momentarily. You come up an hour later and enter our bed like an inexpertly felled pine. In the morning when I wake you're already downstairs with Chris, drinking tea. I hear the dull clack of cups on saucers and your voices, though not your words, filtering through the sanded floorboards.

*

After breakfast we walked along the beach to Aldeburgh. Gulls hung on thermal currents. The breeze blew in warm and the sausage-roll waves flattened and disappeared as the shingle consumed them.

Chris told us the stretch we were walking was part of the "Amber Coast" and that amongst the pebbles lay pieces of Baltic amber transported from forests that, aeons ago, became petrified. Brown resin, he said, had been released from tree trunks and subjected to enormous pressure. An unpolished piece of amber and a smooth brown stone may both look pleasing, Chris added, but it was only the amber, when buffed and held up to the light, that might reveal an inner beauty.

Chris had moved to Suffolk six months after Mum died - five years ago now. A new start, son, he'd said. But there's a room for you. I know you've settled in Brighton, but if you ever change your mind … He ran a kiosk each summer for those in need of ice-creams, sun hats or puzzle books. The rest of the time he walked and played in the Aldeburgh Ukulele Orchestra.

'What kind of music do you like, Emily?'

You rapped out the names of some bands and could see from Chris's face that he'd never heard of any of them. You took a flyer: 'Plus, of course, a few greats: Stevie Wonder, Prince.'

'Now you're talking, Em. We do a couple of Stevie's numbers in the Orchestra.'

'Really?'

Over the next fifteen minutes Chris acquainted us with the company's entire repertoire. His flow was broken only when we passed The Scallop, the beach sculpture dedicated to Benjamin Britten. 'A fine composer and pianist by all accounts …' Chris said, '… but, according to folk-lore, crap on the ukulele.'

We didn't find any pieces of amber yet the weekend trip proved pivotal. You and Chris got on famously: like a hearse on fire he said with a straight face. I think you appreciated his effort to impress and saw honest and good things in him that you suspected might lie a little deeper in me, waiting to be mined and polished.

Chris not only loved us as individuals, he loved us as a couple. In time it became clear that his keenest wish, which he never articulated but which flapped in the air like a sheet on a clothes line, was that we make children - make grandchildren.

Looking back it's not hard to see that, as the foundation for a marriage, it was about as stable as that shingle beach in Suffolk.

Phase Two

Journals chased you, the fattest of the Sunday papers courted you, competition organisers beseeched you to sit on their judging panels. Your collections were drooled over. Chris was your touchstone, that's the way it seemed to me. I think it was because his enthusiasm was unbridled and his raw wit fired yours. By contrast it was obvious I wasn't going to make it as a writer. I was becoming invisible in your glare. That was my conviction. And the aura wasn't confined to your professional life. It flooded the hallways of our relationship. It flowed under the door of any room you were about to enter. And increasingly, when you entered, it was to tell me something I didn't want to hear, or ask me for something I didn't want to give. And I found it was argument that best fitted the contours of my frustration.

In reality my invisibility was bugger-all to do with your glare. I wasn't selling anything. Although I claimed obdurately the opposite I was barely even writing. In the first three years of our middle phase I had one poetry collection published (sales poor), four poems included in obscure anthologies (sales, it seemed, confined to relatives of the contributors), an essay included in a Canadian review (the one that actually paid, thank God) and one short story printed gratis in the monthly magazine of that wildlife charity you supported. My novel progressed like a snail pulling a shed full of obsolete gardening equipment. At the time I said being dropped was a spur; that I'd get another agent – one who earned their cut. I'll say now, it was a mercy.

And so early in that middle phase, I could always find a reason not to go with you to those literary festivals. "The desk beckons," became my fig-leaf phrase. In truth I couldn't endure the experience of you starting the festival audience cheering when my job was starting the car when they'd stopped. So Chris did it, bless him. He chauffeured you to Hay, to Charleston, to Cheltenham, to Oxford. To wherever.

Something had to change and my decision to give up writing professionally and go into advertising with the excuse that it involved some writing, seemed a good move. I'd be a net contributor, I said; professionally valued. You told me I should wait a while longer - hang on for my big break. You had faith in me. You could support us both. That's precisely what I didn't want.

And Chris hated it. Even when I came up with my first successful corporate strap-line and began to be reeled in by, as he termed them, the louterati, even then Chris thought I was breaking ranks. I remember the question, posed with that little half-smile of his that killed me: "But why do you want to go to work on a cliché, son?"

You said you couldn't move from Brighton; it would damage your writing; take you away from your cabal of wise counsellors. So I was commuting to London and had too much time on my hands (as well as my feet). Our troubles began to pick up speed. The cushioning of time says things might have been salvaged had we started a family. But our timetables said we couldn't stop to take on passengers. When eventually, with mismatched enthusiasm, we tried, we found we couldn't. Unanimously, we were ripped open. It wasn't news to be believed until the tests confirmed it was.

I remember when I told Chris he wouldn't be playing the grandfather role - disappointment filled his eyes, his shoulders slumped. For a while he became a smaller man within which a yet smaller man seemed determined to eat his way out. I knew he felt crushed on behalf of everyone involved, including the never-to-be-born.

If I'd lied to Chris about the not-having-kids thing, said we were waiting a while, maybe, just maybe, our second phase wouldn't have been quite so corrosive. Okay, the two of us would have had to contain the devastation between us, but we could've let Chris carry on administering the myrrh of mirth. It would have been a justifiable deceit. Maybe our second phase could have been one of only two. Who knows?

The gravitational force that stretched Phase Two beyond its obvious life-span, that required of it a viscosity it would never otherwise have searched for, was Chris's sadness. You and I couldn't part company while his face was longer than his arm. We made adjustments but we knew they were merely top-coats. Trying to lift Chris had no beneficial side-effects on "us". We commuted and communed, not much else. Eventually, more than a year later, we could detect Chris coming out of it: a chirpiness crept into the odd phone call; a little attitude inveigled its way into the gait. And then you received that email, the one attaching his meta-limerick, asking for feedback. He said he'd rediscovered his mojo. It had been in his ukulele case the whole time.

Phase Three

The moment of silence has grown from awkward to decisive; to the point where, quite clearly, nothing more needs to be said.

'Well I hope you're happy now!' you say, looking out of the window at the rain bouncing off the car roof. I suspect that leaving your umbrella on the back seat was a deliberate act.

In saying you hope I'm happy, you really mean satisfied - satisfied with an outcome of relationship-failure. We both know that was never my wish. And it's not as though you didn't throw a few rocks into the sack that was our marriage. I think what you're really expressing is your despair at relinquishing something you'd been determined not to give up. But a compromise with the pain on only one-side is no compromise: it's either a victory or a defeat depending on your position. And we have definitely reached a compromise – each having won something we say, truthfully, we value and each having given up the one thing which we know is irreplaceable and the loss of which we will forever mourn.

Without turning around you say: 'It's exactly like the downpour when we went to see Chris play. It was this kind of rain: rain that makes you want to take off your floppy hat; rain that feels utterly fantastic running down your face; warm rain.'

Rain that smuggles away tears. You're referring to our day at the Amber Coast Summer Festival three months since. The Aldeburgh Ukulele Orchestra's set finished with Chris's own composition: the song you'd encouraged him to complete; the one you reassured him was visionary. We sat rain-sodden in the front row courtesy of tickets that Chris had sent us months before. Chris had winked at us when the orchestra, seated under a canopy bellied with rainwater, struck up the opening bar of that closing song.

Phase Three then, the shortest of our three phases, would have been even shorter had we not agreed, at your suggestion, to delay our split until after that festival. Our final outing.

The end consists of a mutual acceptance of the situation, the signing of forms and a deal over access to Chris, who aches for us all to remain friends. And now, having signed those forms on a battered desk above which hangs my favourite poem, you walk out into the warm rain.

***

Awaiting the Magnolia
Richard Garcka

The tantrums had become more frequent. Anne heard a crashing sound and put aside her embroidery to see if he needed help. Hurrying down, she felt more like a mother than a wife. The eight-year age gap meant little when they married, but they were young then. As the years passed, he became absorbed in his work and she became more of a nursemaid. Anne sometimes felt there were four children in the house, rather than three. She stopped on the stairs and held her hand against her mouth. There, she'd done it again. Hamnet had died when he was eleven. Even after ten years, her mind sometimes refused to let her remember. Then the memory would re-emerge, like a wave smashing against a rock. Hamnet's twin, Judith, still lived at home with her older sister, Susanna, and Anne knew how lucky she was to have two beautiful daughters. But the loss of her son lurked in a dark corner of her mind, always in the background, ever present.

"Will, are you well? May I enter?" Anne tapped on the oak door of the study. These days, he often worked in London. It was rare for him to spend long at home and Anne suspected it was only the prospect of seeing his daughters that brought him back from time to time. She also wondered who cared for him in London.

There was no answer, so she lifted the latch and pushed against the door. The late afternoon sun cast a patchwork of light through the leaded windows. Strewn across the oak flooring were scraps of parchment, some screwed up, others ripped and shredded, forming a crescent of chaos around the central mahogany desk facing the window. Anne deduced that the more egregious writing, that which had caused the most dissatisfaction, had been cast the furthest. Those scraps of parchment crushed into a ball so they may be flung with greater intensity.

William sat at the desk, his head slumped forward onto his crossed arms, his face turned away from the door. Surveying the room, Anne deduced that his ink pot had recently been thrown with some force at the fireplace, where it had shattered in a display of glass and blue ink, like a field of cornflowers against early morning dew. On a table to one side stood a lunch of bread, cheese and ale, untouched. The manuscripts and folios which lined the shelves of the oak-panelled walls, once ordered and stacked, were pulled at wild angles to complete the scene of desolation.

"Will, are you hurt? Let me help."

He turned his head and looked up without lifting from his arms. His broad forehead showed smears of ink where he'd been rubbing his face with his left hand. Eyes that Anne remembered as once mischievous, were now bloodshot. The moustache and beard had not been trimmed for days, giving him the look of a vagabond. The skin was sallow, unhealthy. Anne had not seen him so distraught and her initial reaction was to withdraw and pull the door shut behind her. But his eyes seemed to call out to her. Her nursing duties were again needed.

"Will, what is it?"

"It's ugliness, Anne. Everything I write is repugnant. The Muses have abandoned me and left this grotesque shell of a playwright. I drown in a sea of hideous mediocrity. I will never write again." With that, he turned his face away, staring at the fire.

"Let me help, my love. Perhaps I might inspire you, like before. Tell me of what you write."

"What's the point, Anne?" William pushed himself into an upright position, arms braced against the edge of the desk as though trying to distance himself from his work. "All is as nothing. I will cease writing and end my days as a jobbing actor, treading the boards of rural theatres like a third-rate jester cast from Court."

Anne had witnessed this melodrama before, but it re-emerged with increasing frequency of late. She knew that William felt pressure to produce the next play. They always wanted more, the audience, the theatre-owners, the Royal Court. The death of Queen Elizabeth two years' ago, after more than forty years on the throne, had caused much uncertainty in the country. With the nervousness around this new King James, people wanted distraction and that meant a growing demand on writers to provide diversions. Four plays in the last two years had been arduous and Anne feared that the burden was too much for William to bear.

"Humour me, my love. Describe your play to me."

"Very well. It concerns an elderly King of Britain, who decides to leave his kingdom to two of his three daughters. The guilt drives him to madness. That part, I can depict." William brushed his hand across the desk, disturbing a pile of parchment with a casual flick. "Aye, the madness of kings I convey with a fine flourish. That should be on my gravestone. Here he lies, the playwright of madmen. Gather round, you fools and simpletons, and marvel at the wit of Stratford's greatest portrayer of lunatics."

"Hush, my love." Anne moved closer and placed her hand over her husband's. He stared at the fire, his mouth fixed and grim, then looked up at her.

"Forgive me, my wife. Only you know the anger that fills me when I cannot complete my work. The Company in London is pressing me for the first draft, but I have no final act."

"My love?"

"The three daughters," he explained, "all die by different

means and it leaves their father, the king, devastated. His life will end too, I am convinced, but I cannot convey his feelings at the loss of his daughters, especially his favourite. I do not have the words in me, Anne. The language teases me like a sprite dancing across the water. As I approach, she darts away. That sense of loss, how do I convey the emotion? I have not the tools. I am but a poor excuse for a writer." Anne saw tears in his eyes as he turned away from her with a grimace.

She knew this lack of confidence to be unmerited. His portrayal of the grieving Moor last year was hailed as a triumph. William's understanding of the human psyche, his instinctive appreciation of human nature, had been what first attracted Anne to him when he was still a youth. It was an extraordinary gift for one so young, a maturity beyond his years. That uncanny ability still existed; she was sure. He needed to rediscover the part of him that lifted the veil of mankind's thoughts and passions. That facility for insight that drew the audiences into his theatres in their hundreds.

"Walk with me, my love. Perhaps the cool air will revitalise your spirits." She lifted his hand and drew him to his feet. William followed without speaking, lost in his dark mood. Anne guided him out of the study and through the parlour to the rear of the house, where a door led into a garden. Their house was surrounded by a cottage garden on three sides, with vegetables growing on the other. Pottering in the garden was one of Anne's pleasures. Few came to visit in Stratford. Most of William's close friends were in London. When the girls were away visiting relatives, as they were now, Anne spent a lot of time alone. She had become attached to her flowers and took pride in her garden.

She steered William down the path and through a rickety gate at the end. Their garden backed onto a small copse and they walked along a narrow track. It was April and the first daffodils were open, dancing in the late afternoon breeze.

Too early yet for the bluebells, but trees and shrubs displayed their buds as though responding to the daffodil's call – we see you and will join soon. With the path so narrow, winding through swaying ferns carpeting the floor, William followed behind, pulled along like a tired pony.

They arrived at a clearing, a patch of open land so circular as to appear man-made, though Anne knew that the trees had been felled here by a local farmer some years back. The symmetry of the circle, of a circumference that would take less than a minute to walk, lent it an otherworldly feel. If you were unaware of the hand of man, you might think it the work of elves and fairies, a secret grotto of magic and wonder.

Anne held with none of that nonsense. Sprites and spirits did not exist in her world, even though they would often play a part in William's plays. Anne was of the here and now. Nature for her did not require the embellishment of fanciful creatures to augment its beauty. She led William over to the far side of the circle and encouraged him to sit with her beside a magnolia bush.

The magnolia was in full bloom. A dazzling vision of white flowers like cupped hands impeaching the sky. The scent subtle, not overwhelming like a rose, but teasing, elusive, a half-opened door offering a glimpse of a promise.

"This is my favourite spot to sit in the early Spring," said Anne, leaning back onto her straightened arms, looking up at the blossom hanging over them. William stared about, unfocused, distracted.

"What's so special about it, my dear? There is little here to lift the spirits."

"Look up, Will. The magnolia blossom lasts for just a few short weeks before the winds and April rains take their toll." She closed her eyes as though trying to imprint the memory of the blossom in her mind before it departed. "Beauty in this world can be so fleeting. Sunlight striking a stream creates more colours than you knew existed, all to be snuffed out by a passing cloud. A family of deer in a glade, alert, watchful, full of life, vanish when startled by the hunter's tread. Or the magnolia's blossom." Anne opened her eyes again and look across to her husband. "All year, the tree mourns the loss of its colour, then it returns and reminds us of what we once loved."

William sat up, looked up at the blossom, then across to Anne, his eyes widened as he understood what she was saying, then he looked down, saddened.

"You're speaking of Hamnet."

"I miss him so much, Will. His earnest face. The way he walked. His little laugh. I sit beneath the magnolia, awaiting the return of the blossom, when I can be reminded of our beautiful boy. And then the petals are gone, stolen from us. And I must wait another year."

William covered his face with his hands, then breathed in deeply and rose to his feet. He reached down and lifted Anne up before taking her in his arms.

"My darling wife. I am but a dullard in your presence. It is you who should be inscribing the words that bring tears and laughter to the audience. I too miss our son. I had forgotten the way he would look at me with those round eyes. Such a soft voice. I remember wishing that heaven would crack…"

They held each other for a while, then set off back to the cottage.

"I believe I can complete the final act, my love."

"I knew you would, my husband. I would only ask, make no mention of the magnolia. Let that be our secret."

William looked at her.

"I promise you, Anne. I will never write of the magnolia.

54

That belongs to us and no-one else."

Anne walked back with her husband as the sun dipped below the trees leaving the clearing in a twilight gloom that only the blossom of the magnolia could penetrate.

Fate's Children
Diana Alexander

There was something curious about the kingdom of
Amaranth. It wasn't something your average stranger would
spot right away, however. The sun rose in the east and set in
the west. The houses all had walls and ceilings and windows.
No, the peculiar thing about Amaranth had to do with its
people. Most Amarantheans came into the world, lived
eighty or so years, and then passed on to whatever came
next. That is to say, most were mortal. Most, but not all.
You see, a small number, maybe one in a thousand, were
born with the gift of immortality. There were many theories
as to why this happened, but most agreed that the granting
of this gift appeared to be left entirely to chance. It did not
matter if a child's parents were both immortals or if their
entire family tree was filled with mortals. They were just as
likely to be untouched by time. It was not a gift granted only
to the good, or to the brave or the wise, for there were many
kinds of immortals, both kind and cruel.

As you would imagine, these circumstances led to many a
quandary in the kingdom. If the heir to the throne turned
out to be an immortal, would they reign forever? If an
immortal committed a terrible crime that came with a
punishment of life in prison, was it right to keep them
locked away for eternity?

It must be said that though these chosen few were called
immortals, this was a slight misnomer, for while they would
never age, they were not completely invulnerable. There
were three things rumored to be able to end the life of an
immortal, but these were so rare that they were almost
forgotten. The first was dragonfire. The second was the
sting of a silver bee. Finally, there were certain weapons,
forged thousands of years ago, that legend said could kill
anything in existence. Dragons rarely interacted with

humankind and preferred to stay in their mountain dens. There had not been a recorded sighting of a silver bee in almost a century, and most Amarantheans considered celestial weapons to be more myth than fact. Therefore, for all intents and purposes, the immortals could never die.

In the Amaranthean town of Dell, squeezed between a fishmonger and an apothecary, there stood an orphanage. Magna Mater Home for Foundlings had been built many centuries ago and it was clear from the crumbling brick and dilapidated roof that its peak had long since passed. However, the children within its walls were kept clean and well fed. They were given three hearty meals a day, drawn regular baths, and taught to read and write. The twins Palla and Cat had lived at Magna Mater since they had been found on a bitter winter's night, half frozen and clinging to each other for warmth. They had been brought to the orphanage, given a warm meal and a bed, and there they had remained. The best that the matrons could figure, the pair had been abandoned and left to fend for themselves on the streets of Dell. Since arriving at Magna Mater, the siblings had been nearly inseparable. Though they shared the same dark hair and wide hazel eyes, their natures were very different. Palla was forever getting into trouble with her sharp tongue and impetuousness, but she was always ready to defend those weaker than herself. More often than not, this included her brother. Unlike his twin, Cat endeavored to avoid confrontation at all costs. He preferred to hole up in the dusty library and read his way through Magna Mater's sizable collection of books. Despite their contrarieties, the siblings together made the perfect team. Palla's rough edges were softened under Cat's influence, and Cat became more outgoing when his sister was at his side.

The caretaker of their ward was an immortal called Matron Penelope, who, though she had been alive several centuries, looked barely older than some of her charges. Sometimes, on particularly stormy nights when the children were restless, she would tell them tales of the many strange and wonderful things she had seen. Fantastic stories of great battles and amazing creatures in faraway lands. Palla and Cat had always listened with wide eyed wonder. Palla was particularly enthralled and took every opportunity to wring details out of the matron.

"But if you are an immortal," she began one day while the brother and sister were helping with the washing up after dinner, "why do you stay here at Magna Mater? You could go anywhere, do anything."

A faraway look had appeared on Matron Penelope's kind, youthful face at these words. For a second, the twins imagined they could see the centuries reflected in her clear eyes as she looked out the kitchen window.

"I once thought like you did, Palla. When I first began to suspect I was an immortal, I was overjoyed. The world was at my fingertips. I left on grand adventures, sought out the answers to life's mysteries. Years passed, and the people around me began to grow old. Time had stood still for me, but not for the people I loved. First my parents. Then my husband, my siblings, finally my children." In response to the startled looks on their faces, she had smiled sadly. "Yes, I had two children, long ago. They were twins like you. My little girls. They grew up, had families of their own. When my grandchildren's children passed to the afterworld, I decided to depart and watch over my descendants from afar instead. Love had just become too painful."

"What happened then, Matron?" Palla had asked eagerly.

"Then I left for the coast and built myself a little cottage on the beach as far from...well, as far from everything and everyone as I could get. I only had myself for a companion and it was terribly lonely, but at least my heart was protected. Many immortals end up exiling themselves sooner or later, you know. They become weary of the world

59

and all its death and pain. They begin to think of their immortality as a curse rather than a gift."

"But you didn't stay there, did you Matron," Cat had prompted, so absorbed in the tale that he hadn't noticed the front of his shirt was dripping with soapy water.

"No. It took many decades, but I finally realized that I could be doing so much more with the time that had been given to me. Instead of wallowing in despair over life's sorrows, I should be trying to ease them. So, one day I packed up my belongings and set out for Magna Mater to raise children to whom fate had been cruel." She spread her robed arms wide. "And here I am."

Young Palla had scrunched up her nose then. "That was a sad story." she said. "I only like stories with happy endings." She scrubbed a plate vigorously with a sponge. "If I was an immortal, I would try to climb to the top of the tallest mountain or...or steal all the gold and jewels in the world."

Her brother had shaken his head fervently at this. "Not me. That sounds too scary. I think I would become a scholar and read all the books in the Great Library."

"Oh, come on, Cat," Palla had said exasperatedly, rolling her eyes. "You would be an immortal. That means you couldn't die. There would be nothing to be afraid of." She turned to Matron Penelope. "Do you think maybe we could be immortals, Cat and me?"

Matron Penelope had looked thoughtful at this question, waiting to reply until she had finished drying the cup in her hand. When she did answer, she spoke slowly, as if choosing her words carefully. "The odds are incredibly slim that even one of you is an immortal, let alone both. At your age, it is almost impossible to determine. The only ways to know for sure are to survive a mortal wound and live, or if the years pass and you do not age." She opened her mouth to continue, then closed it again abruptly as if thinking better of what she was about to say.

"What is it Matron?"

"Well, that is…. what you need to understand…" Clearly wishing she had let the subject drop, Matron Penelope had sighed deeply. "I was going to tell of another way, but very few ever make it to the presence of the Oracle. Those who do often learn that some questions are better left unanswered. No, best to leave that path alone. Now, off to bed both of you, or Matron Selene will give us all a scolding."

The years passed, and life at Magna Mater went on as it had done for centuries. Foundlings entered its aegis and left it. There had been a terrible winter where several of the children had succumbed to the Delirian Flu. Palla and Cat had both made it through untouched, but many of their friends had not survived to reach the spring. The twins had grown to be healthy and resourceful under the stern but kind care of the matrons. Though there had been opportunities for one or the other to be adopted by a family, they had always refused to be parted, and so they had remained at Magna Mater.

As they approached their sixteenth birthday, it became time to plan for their future. It was custom that when a foundling reached this age, they would be given a few gold coins, a map, and two weeks food rations. They were expected to go out into the world and seek their fortune. Many found work in Dell as apprentices or took the longer, more dangerous journey to the royal city where there were more opportunities for work. Palla and Cat had spent many an hour discussing what they should do once they left Magna Mater, but could not come to a decision. They still did not know if either was an immortal, and they were terrified at the possibility that they might be left one day to face the rest of eternity alone.

Finally, having had enough of being paralyzed by uncertainty, the brother and sister resolved to find out the truth, whatever the cost. Remembering what Matron Penelope had said in their childhood, they went to her a fortnight before their departure to request her help in finding the Oracle. The matron had not aged a day in all the years she had looked after them. Her hair was still as golden as wheat, and her face remained unlined. When they put the question to her, she looked troubled but unsurprised.

"I thought you might ask this one day," she said. "Are you sure this is what you want? Wouldn't it be better to leave this question to be answered in the natural progression of time?"

The brother and sister looked at each other, then shook their heads in identical gestures. Palla, as usual, was the first to speak. "We've been together our whole lives, Matron, since even before we were born. When we were on the streets, we only had each other to rely on. Cat and I are two halves of a whole. We've agreed that the only way we're going to be able to move forward with our lives is if we know what the future holds." She looked into her brother's face, so similar to her own. "If we're both mortal, so be it. After we die, we'll meet again one day in the afterworld. If we're both immortal, we can spend the rest of eternity having adventures together. If one of us is mortal and the other immortal...well, I guess I don't know what we'll do then. I can't bear the thought that we could be separated forever. It would be like losing part of myself."

The matron took a moment to consider Palla's words, then shook her head slowly. "I understand your reasons, but I cannot help you. Amarantheans far older and wiser than you have ruined their lives because they misinterpreted a prophecy. I will not aid in ruining yours. Heed my words. The Oracle brings only misfortune, even if it wears the guise of truth."

On the morning of their sixteenth birthday, as the sun rose above the rooftops of Dell, the twins waved goodbye to the matrons and set out on the road leading toward the distant mountains. Since Matron Penelope's refusal to help them, Cat had spent all of the intervening time in the library searching for some mention of the location of the Oracle. Finally, he had found a small paragraph in a book entitled Interpreting the Divine that gave the information they sought. Since then, he and Palla had been planning their journey in secret, all the while putting forth the story that they intended to travel to the royal city.

Never having left the town before, Palla had wanted to take the meandering, enigmatic road through the forest. Cat, fearing bandits and bloodthirsty creatures, had convinced her that the royal thoroughfare would be safer, as it skirted the borders of the forest and was well patrolled. Three days after leaving Magna Mater, the pair were rewarded with their first view of their destination as hazy peaks began to rise above the tree line. Another two days found them crossing a narrow bridge that spanned over a deep gorge at the foot of the largest mountain. Its rocky slopes were dotted in flowers the color of rubies that seemed to almost burn in the bright sunlight.

As they stepped off the last wooden plank of the bridge, the twins were faced with the entrance to a yawning cave. It had an unsettling resemblance to a giant maw ready to swallow them whole. The only signs that this was the dwelling of the Oracle were some ancient carved symbols around the edge that even Cat couldn't read. They tried to peer inside, but the darkness was impenetrable.

"You don't think there's a back door, do you?" asked Cat nervously.

Palla rolled her eyes. "We've come all this way, Cat. Take a risk for once in your life. You know I'll have your back."

Cat sighed. Palla was always able to convince him to do things against his better judgement. "Fine," he muttered, "but when we get killed, I'll be expecting a heartfelt apology."

Palla led the way as they slowly descended into the darkness. Their footsteps echoed loudly in the cool, damp tunnel. Cat, following behind his sister, touched the rough walls and felt words and designs etched there, though he could not see them. He wished desperately that they had thought to bring matches. Even the smallest sounds were making him jump, and he felt as if unseen eyes were watching them as they made their way blindly forward.

After twenty minutes or so of walking, the darkness began to lighten almost imperceptibly. Palla was the first to notice. She stopped abruptly. Cat, who had been focusing on making as little noise as possible and therefore had not observed any change, ran into her.

"Ouch," he said. "Why'd you stop?"

Palla reached out and grabbed his hand tightly. "Look," she said, "I can see a light. I think we're almost there."

Cat squinted into the gloom. There did indeed seem to be a sort of glow ahead. As they crept closer, a strong smell like incense flooded their noses. It was thick and had a soporific effect to it. Palla and Cat suddenly realized how very weary they were after their journey, but both fought hard to stay alert. They would need to keep their wits about them.

Exiting the tunnel, the siblings stepped into a large, cavernous room supported by two rows of gargantuan stone pillars. They immediately located the source of the light, a large basin balanced on a pedestal and filled with brilliant orange flames. The firelight cast dancing, flickering shadows in every corner of the cavern, tricking the eyes into believing the room was filled with writhing figures. Standing behind the pedestal was a tall, hooded figure.

Oh, I don't like this, thought Cat. Fantastic, thought Palla. As the twins cautiously approached the basin, the figure spoke.

"Welcome travelers," the sentinel said in a whisper as soft as rustling leaves. "State your purpose in coming to this sacred place."

Palla stepped forward. "My name is Palla, and this is my brother Cat. We wish to consult the Oracle...your giftsPlease," she added hastily as Cat elbowed her in the ribs.

The sentinel stood silent. Cat got the impression that they were being considered, though he could not see the figure's face. He shifted his weight from foot to foot restlessly. A minute longer and the whisper came again.

"Very well. You will need to make an offering in the basin, and we shall see if the gods accept your gift."

As they had been advised in the book, the twins drew out one of their small sacks of gold and remaining food rations from their packs, then cast them into the flames. For a second, nothing happened. Then, without warning, the fire flared into a towering inferno that nearly reached the ceiling of the cavern. A moment later, the flames dimmed, allowing them to see that their offerings were gone.

"It seems that the gods are pleased with your gifts," the sentinel said. He raised a hand and snapped his fingers. The doors on the other end of the cavern swung open silently.

The room they entered was hazy and dimly lit. They could tell instantly that this was the origin of the incense smell they had noted earlier. Seated on a dais in the middle of the room was a woman clothed in a flowing white dress. Her skin was dark and luminous, and beneath her curls rested a golden circlet. At last, they had reached the Oracle. Palla and Cat, side by side, approached the dais.

The Oracle's eyes were closed. When they knelt in front of

her, she spoke in a low, clear voice that echoed in the small room. "Greetings my children. What truth do you seek?"

Palla took a deep breath. "My lady, we wish to know if we will someday be parted by death." She paused, then cleared her throat awkwardly. Matron Penelope had told them that the Oracle was easy to misinterpret and she wanted to leave no room for doubt. "Do you think you could make your answer a bit...er... more straightforward than usual?"

"Palla," hissed Cat. Everyone knew the Oracle was an instrument of the gods, and it was not wise to enrage the divine.

The Oracle, however, did not appear offended. On the contrary, she looked faintly amused. "You have spirit, daughter. Good, you will need it. Very well. I will honor your request." She stood and descended from the dais, her eyes still closed. Her ivory dress glided behind her as she approached.

As she stood in front of the siblings, the Oracle held out her hands and placed one on each of their foreheads. Her lids flew open, revealing her eyes to be entirely white. "I see," she said in a rasping voice, quite unlike the one she had greeted them with. "I see that one of you will long outlive the other." Before they had a chance to let this sink in, the Oracle pressed both of her palms to Palla's forehead, who felt them searing her skin.

"You were born a mortal, my daughter." Arms still outstretched, she turned to Cat and repeated the action.

"You were born an immortal, my son." The Oracle's arms dropped to her sides and her eyes closed once again. The brother and sister looked at each other, their worst fears confirmed. They would indeed be parted. Perhaps it would not be for fifty, sixty, even seventy years or so, but they would someday be torn apart and there was nothing they could do about it.

Palla and Cat exited the cave and stepped into the sunlight. They blinked rapidly as their eyes adjusted from the darkness. When their vision cleared, they saw their own emotions mirrored on the other's face. Tears were rolling down both their cheeks, and their hazel eyes were puffy and red. Without speaking, they walked away from the cave and lay down side by side in the shadow of a large Juniper tree. There was silence between them for a time, with each lost in their own thoughts. Finally, Cat voiced the one that was foremost on both their minds.

"I don't want to be alone."

Though Palla had never felt less like smiling, she forced one for her brother's sake. "Cheer up Cat," she said, making her tone as light as possible. "I'm not dead yet. We'll just have to enjoy the time we have left together, that's all. When I die, you'll watch over my children, and my children's children and my grandchildren's children." Her chin trembled a bit, but she turned her head the other way so Cat wouldn't notice. More than ever, she needed to be strong for both of them. "See, you won't ever be alone." Cat said nothing, so Palla went on. "Look at it this way. You're an immortal. Think of all the things you will be able to do and see. You don't have to be afraid of anything anymore." She let her voice trail away. Her brother had not given any indication that he had heard her words. "Cat?" she asked. "You there?"

Lying on the ground next to his sister and staring up at the clouds, Cat had been imagining his life stretching before him, endless and bleak, the years bleeding into centuries. At that moment, it seemed unbearable.

"Cat? You there?"

Stop it, he thought fiercely. Pull it together. For Palla. She's not as strong as she pretends to be. He forced himself to picture living out one of Matron Penelope's stories instead, sailing on a pirate ship to the ends of the earth or joining an expedition to the jungle. He would have all the time in the world to study and learn and explore. Sitting up, he wiped his eyes hurriedly with his sleeve and cleared his throat. "You're right," he said, his voice hoarse. "Maybe I've been looking at this all wrong. Instead of a curse, maybe immortality could be a gift." Cat smiled slightly as his sister sat up as well and leaned against the tree, her arms wrapped around her knees. "You know better than anyone that I've never been very brave, but now I can protect you like I never could as a child. I can make sure that we never have to be scared and helpless ever again." He glanced upwards toward a small plateau further up the mountain. What little they could see of it was covered in those beautiful crimson flowers they had noticed on their way to the Oracle. A light came into his eyes. "I'll prove it by bringing back one of those flowers you liked so much."

Cat got to his feet, gave his sister a reassuring smile, then walked to the craggy mountainside. His fingers found natural handholds in the rock, and he began to hoist himself upwards. Palla, sitting in the shadow of the tree, watched her twin scale the steep mountainside with apprehension in the pit of her stomach. Though she knew now that Cat was an immortal and was in no real danger, it was still in her nature to be worried about him. She had been protecting him their whole lives. That was going to be a hard habit to break. She watched as Cat reached the ledge and pulled himself up and over. His voice drifted down faintly. "Palla. You should see it. It's so beautiful." Palla heard a note of exhilaration in his voice that had never been there before.

On top of the plateau, Cat was surveying the breathtaking view. Amaranth was stretched out before him. Rivers and hills and dales extended as far as he could see. It was just starting to sink in that he had eternity to sojourn each and every one if he chose. He felt an ache of sadness that Palla would not always be there next to him, but he pushed this thought aside. Like she had said, that day was far in the future. He stretched out a hand to pick one of the hundreds of crimson flowers at his feet. He would bring one back to his sister as a sign that she did not need to worry about him anymore. As his fingers touched the silky petals, he felt a prick of pain. Damn, a thorn, he thought.

Palla was peering upwards to where her brother had disappeared over the edge of the plateau. It had been thirty minutes since he had made the ascent and he had not responded to her shouted demands to know what was taking so long up there. Fifteen minutes more and Palla was beginning to get genuinely worried. She decided that, despite the steep drop, she was going to follow her brother up the mountainside. She gripped the rough handholds and began the ascent.

As Palla pulled herself over the ledge just as Cat had done, her first observation was of the beautiful patchwork the green grass and the blood red flowers made. Her second was of Cat lying in this sea of color, a flower grasped in one of his hands. His eyes were closed and there was a serene expression on his face. Palla let out a sigh of relief. Of course. Cat had fallen asleep. He always could sleep in the strangest places. She called his name, but Cat did not stir. She walked over and knelt down, shaking his shoulder gently. When he still did not wake, she shook him harder. "Cat!" she yelled, panicked now. "Wake up." Tears that had been so close to the surface since they had left the Oracle now began to spill over. "Cat," she whispered.

A flash out of the corner of her eye made her look up. A small insect, no bigger than her thumbnail, was fluttering above their heads. Its sterling wings glittered in the sunlight as it flew. Though she had never seen one except in drawings, Palla knew instantly what it was. A silver bee. She watched as it landed on a crimson flower, then took flight once more. She turned back to Cat. No, this couldn't be. It was wrong, all wrong. Cat couldn't be dead. She was the one who was supposed to go to the afterworld first, not him. Palla thought back desperately to the words of the Oracle. "I see that one of you will long outlive the other." She hadn't actually revealed which twin that would be, however. They had simply taken it for granted that it would be Cat. "You were born an immortal, my son." But she hadn't said that he would live forever.

Palla took Cat's familiar hand, which was colder than it had been in life. She bowed her head to her brother's side, letting her tears fall on his chest. As she wept, she wished bitterly that they had never come to this place. She knew now why Matron Penelope had warned them against taking this path. The Oracle had given them exactly what they had asked for, but that knowledge had come at a terrible price.

The Woman in the Grey Coat
Liz Diamond

The first time I saw the woman in the grey coat I was
waiting for the train to London Euston. I was on my way to
meet Jack. The woman was standing a bit further down the
platform from me as the train pulled into Watford Junction.
There were other people in between us: a man in a navy-
blue coat; a young mum with a toddler whining in a
pushchair; a teenage girl wearing red heels and a short black
skirt, who looked like she was on her way to a party despite
it being eleven o'clock on a Saturday morning. But what
made me notice the woman in the grey coat, what drew me
to her, was the fact that she looked very like an older
version of myself. She was my height, but plumper than I
am, and she had a face shaped very like mine, but sadder.
More lined, and fallen around the jowls so that her mouth
was down-turned as if her life had dealt her too many
disappointments.

You know that feeling you have when you see someone you
don't know and yet you feel as if you know them, you've
met them before? Well, it was like that. A kind of deja vu. I
didn't speak to her on that occasion, I didn't get a chance to.
The train pulled in and people got off from different
carriages so that soon there were more than a few people
between us, there were many, and the woman drifted down
the platform, as if she was looking for a particular carriage
to enter, and yet looking at the same time as though she
wasn't looking for anything at all. I watched her for a while,
and then she disappeared from sight and I got on the train
at Carriage G and found an empty seat next to the window.

Jack and I went to see an exhibition at Tate Modern. It was
an installation of sculptures of bodies formed from wire
mesh pinpricked with tiny LED lights. I couldn't decide if I
liked it or not. The wire mesh, the space between the points

71

of light, made the bodies up-close look insubstantial, empty. But from a distance it was strangely compelling, although disconcerting. Perhaps we are all like that, I thought, looking at the lights in the vastness of the exhibition hall. Pinpricks of light in space. Nothing more.

The weather was cool, especially for early June, and every so often a thin scattering of rain fell; it quite spoilt our plans to get the tube to St James Park and eat the sandwiches we had bought, so we decided to go to a cafe for lunch in Convent Market. Only I had forgotten how expensive it can be there; the spinach and ricotta flan I ordered was tired when it arrived; the lettuce in the side salad wilted and warm, the beetroot relish a tad too acidic. And then it started to rain much harder and we decided not to bother with the Imperial War Museum but to catch the tube straight to Jack's place instead.

Just small niggles, small disappointments. But with hindsight now it feels as if they were setting the stage for the bigger one that happened later at Jack's flat that evening.

Jack and I had been going out together for about six months now. He was a trainee solicitor with a firm based in Harrow. We'd met at the party of a mutual friend who lived in Watford. It was the first relationship I'd had for three years that had gone that sort of distance and I guess I was expecting some discussion, maybe even that evening, about moving things up to the next notch. Jack shared a flat in Harrow Wealdstone with another young solicitor, who had arranged to be out that evening at his girlfriend's, mainly on account of my staying over, and I lived with two other professional women - Chloe, who taught primary age kids, and Shona, a nurse in elderly care - in a terraced property in North Watford. Being a self-employed aroma-therapist, it wouldn't be difficult for me to relocate to North London, and maybe even advantageous from the point of view of securing a solid client base, so I was up for that kind of 'let's start thinking about moving in together' kind of talk.

But that wasn't what I got. We'd eaten first. Jack had cooked. He was a good cook on the whole, having gleaned much of his knowledge from watching Master-chef and reading Jamie Oliver cookbooks. We had cod with a herb crust served on a bed of Mediterranean vegetables and quinoa, which was an interesting blend of the soft with the crunchy. We polished off one bottle of wine and then got started on another. Then we actually went to bed and made love, spurred on no doubt by the wine. Afterwards, we both got up again and downloaded a film to watch. The film was really more my choice than Jack's, women bonding with other women and too much chat for him. He became restless and fiddled with his phone a bit. Then he asked if I'd mind if we turned the telly off because he'd something important to tell me.

So that was when I got the big disappointment. The one all those small niggles of the day had been leading towards. He'd got that job he'd applied for, he said. I'd almost forgotten he had applied for another job; he had to remind me. Perhaps I'd been in denial, blotting it out. But yes, of course. A job in Manchester. Closer to his roots, to his home town. Jack came from a village in Cheshire. Maybe I hadn't thought he'd get it. Or maybe I didn't think he'd go through with it if he did. But apparently he'd received a letter from them yesterday and he'd already written back his response. He was accepting the post. It was a promotion. He'd have his own office, his own secretary. He wouldn't be an 'assistant to' but the co-partner of the firm. They specialised in criminal casework. It was exciting, what he'd been working towards for such a long time. A new beginning. But one he thought best to make on his own, unencumbered. Time to call a halt on things, perhaps, have time out. From Us, that is. We could stay in touch. Maybe when he was more settled I could come and visit for a weekend. See how we felt. See how the land lay.

Perhaps I shouldn't have been so huffy about it. Turned a cold shoulder on him in bed. Refused to make love a second time when he turned to me in the small hours feeling horny again. I grunted, nudged him off. Tried to pretend I was too tired, had a headache. Anything. In the morning I made some excuse about needing to rush off. I'd promised my cousin, Janette, I'd visit her that day, I told him. She was expecting me for lunch. I had to go home first, feed the cat. I didn't even let him kiss me goodbye. Not really. Just a cursory brush of the lips.

I was hurt, I suppose. No, more than that. Devastated, really. Gutted. There was me planning on moving in with him and there was he, planning on sailing off to Manchester without me. Saying goodbye.

It wasn't true about Janette. She wasn't expecting me. I had no plans on at all. If I'm honest, I'd been hoping to spend much of the day with Jack. But not now. Instead, I went back to my terraced house in North Watford - both Shona and Chloe were out - and I went to bed with the cat and wept copiously into her soft fur. Sounds pathetic I know, but I did. It continued to rain, it rained all day, and then Shona came home and thinking I was ill, offered to cook for me. I got up and wrapped myself up in a blanket on the sofa and we watched the omnibus versions of the soaps together, and ate spaghetti with pesto and grated cheddar, followed by brownies and Greek yoghurt, which is just about the best way of spending a Sunday evening on a rainy day in June when your boyfriend's just dumped you.

I guess I got over it. Or thought I had. It didn't take that long. A couple of weeks. Then one evening I was having a bath and planning to go out with Chloe, whose boyfriend was bringing a mate along - a tacit way of arranging a blind date for me - when I suddenly realised I was late. My period, that is. A week late.

I'm never late, not usually, and I supposed I managed to

74

shrug it off, put it down maybe to the stress of the break-up. I went on that blind-date that wasn't a blind-date. He was nice, the guy who was brought along to make up the numbers and meet me. Maybe not earth-shattering nice, but nice. He had a pleasant face. A dimple on his left cheek when he smiled, which was often, and an endearing gap between his front teeth. He used to be in the Royal Engineer Corps, but now was a PE teacher, and under his well fitted jeans and teeshirt it was obvious he had a very good body.

We didn't make definite plans to meet again but he gave me his phone number and I tucked it into the back of my purse where I put important receipts. So the intention was there on the part of both of us. For the next few days I kept itching to take it out and phone him, but I didn't. My period still didn't come and its absence hung over me like the sword of Damocles.

I hadn't got Jack to wear a condom when we'd made love at his flat that Saturday night just before he told me he was dumping me. I'd worked out my dates be-fore going to meet him and decided it was safe so I'd told him not to bother. Actually, it was only on the edge of being safe, only a couple of days outside the 'un-safe' zone. But I was usually very regular, like clockwork, so it felt safe enough. Maybe I was taking a risk. Maybe I didn't think the risk was too great. I'd thought we were an item, with a future to look forward to.

But everything changed. When you're not sure of something, not sure which direction your future will go in, in limbo land so to speak, it's not easy to enjoy the present. It's difficult to make plans, for a start, and without plans it feels like there is no future, and without a future what do you have? I spent a few days like that, restless, not sleeping well, checking all the time for the elusive period that never came. So in the end I gave in and bought one of those pregnancy kits from Boots. You know the kind. The ones with the little blue line. The line of destiny. That's what it felt like to me, anyway, pacing backwards and forwards on the tiled floor of our bathroom waiting for the allotted time to pass.

It turned blue. I stared at the blue for quite some time, my brain willing it to be another colour instead. The pink it had started out to be, or at least a shade of green: orange, burgundy, anything but blue. But it was blue. A nice mid-tone blue, like the sky on a summer's day. There was no mistaking it.

Afterwards I sat down and watched some rubbish on the telly. I don't even re-member what it was. One of the soaps or those silly quizzes where people haven't really a chance in heaven of carrying home money. I felt all the time as if I should be ringing somebody. My mum. My best friend, Chantelle, who lives in Peterborough where I grew up. My cousin, Janette. Jack, even. But I couldn't. What would I say? I'm pregnant. There is a baby growing inside me but I don't know if I shall keep it. I can't bear yet to think of it as a real. Eyes forming, ears. Tiny limbs pushing out. But I wanted you to know about it anyway…

But I did go and tell Jack about it eventually. It was a week later. I phoned him on his mobile. I expected him to already be in Manchester but he said he was still tidying up loose ends in London; the date of him starting his new job had been postponed for a couple of weeks. I said I needed to see him. Could he meet me at Euston Station? He tried to make me tell him what it was, or at least give him hints. But I wouldn't.

"Wait till Saturday," I said

That's when I saw the woman again. The one in the grey coat. She was on the train this time, sitting in carriage D. I passed her whilst edging my way down the aisle to E because there were no window seats left in 'D'. She was sitting in one of the last rows in the carriage, just before you get to that swaying, rattling junction between the carriages. She had one of those small portable suitcases stuck out into the aisle and I nearly tripped over it.

'Oh, sorry," I said, as if it was my fault, lurching forward and grabbing on to the back of the seat opposite her to steady myself. She gave me a brief look that seemed more accusatory than apologetic and edged the suitcase in so that it was more under the seat in front of her.

"You need to be careful," she said. Muttered really. I almost didn't catch it.

"Pardon?" I said.

She looked up at me steadily. She looked a little older than when I'd first seen her at the platform, although I hadn't got a very good look at her then. Her eyes were the same greeny hazel colour as mine. Deep lines etched down from her mouth.

"You need to think it through very carefully," she said. "There'll be no going back." She didn't mutter this time. She spoke quite clearly. Then she looked away. Someone was behind me, clucking impatiently, and I had to go on. I found an empty window seat at the start of the next carriage and sat down.

Did I imagine it? Did she really say that? You need to think it through carefully. There'll be no going back. We passed through a tunnel and I glanced at myself in the window of the train. The darkness behind the glass made it reflect my face almost as clearly as a mirror does. A young, smooth, unlined face, dark hair. There were no sad, downward-drooping lines about my mouth, but in thirty years' time might I, too, look like she does?

My hands instinctively went to my abdomen and rested there.

A little later on I stood up and made my way towards the toilet which was positioned in that rattling space between the two carriages. But before using it, I glanced into carriage D towards the seat where the woman in the grey coat had been sitting. I should have seen the back of her head but instead I saw nothing. The seat was empty. This startled me, because the train had not stopped anywhere, between the moment of my tripping over her case and my looking now for the back of her head.

She must have moved to another carriage, I told myself.

Jack was already waiting for me when I got to the Costa Coffee place at Euston station. He was sipping a cappuccino and had a faint moustache of foam on his upper lip. He stood up, and bent to kiss me in a somewhat feigned, trying-too-hard manner, but I averted my face so his lips slide off my cheek.

"I'll get you a coffee. Skinny latte, as usual?"

I nodded. He came back, a few minutes later, with the latte. Put it down on the table in front of me, sat down, picked up his own.

"Well, how are you? You're looking well," he said. "Sorry I haven't phoned you. They're piling the work on me, now they know I'm leaving."

"That's all right," I said, thinking, you're not supposed to keep ringing people when you've dumped them, anyway. "Have you found somewhere to live in Manchester?" I asked, trying to make my voice sound neutral.

"I'm moving in with an old University mate. Initially, anyway. He's been working in Manchester since Uni days. He's bought his own flat - needs help paying the mortgage. It'll do till I get on my feet."

"I see," I said.

I did see. Jack was clearly striking out on his own, making a new start. New job, new place. No doubt, soon to be new girlfriend. He didn't want any baggage. Clearly, I was baggage. And what I was about to tell him, even more so. Unwanted baggage.

We sat in a sort of awkward silence for a short while. He cleared his throat, ducked his head down towards me.

"I'm sorry, Lisa," he said.

"What are you sorry for?" Did he hear the slight catch in my throat?

"I got us wrong, maybe. I always felt we were casual about things. You know, one of those transitional relationships ..."

"You mean, while we were waiting for something better to come along ..."

He winced. "No, of course not. It's just that I wasn't ready for anything too permanent. I was very fond of you, you know I was."

Was? So I had already relegated to past tense. Unwanted baggage.

"You make me sound like a cat," I said tersely.

"Sorry," he said, again. Another awkward silence. I didn't know what to do anymore. Should I tell him, or should I just walk away? I could feel tears starting to prick my eyes. I'm going to cry in a minute, I thought. And then everything else will be lost.

"Is that what you wanted to talk about, Lisa?"

"What?"

"Us. A second chance. Were you hoping you could change my mind?"

I looked at him. I could sense that he was almost enjoying this. She is here to plead with me, to make me change my mind. There was heat in my face. I wasn't afraid of crying now. I wouldn't give him the satisfaction. I stood up, picked up my bag.

"You haven't finished your latte," he said, in surprise.

"No, Jack. I haven't come here to ask for a second chance. I've come here to tell you that this 'casual thing' between us has started off another life. But I do realise it's very inconvenient for you right now. I certainly wouldn't want it to deter you from your bright new future in Manchester."

I turned and walked off, sharply. I felt his chair scrape on the pavement, his foot-steps running behind me. His hand on my arm, stopping me in my tracks.

"Look, Lisa. I didn't know. You should've said on the phone. You should've warned me."

I turned and looked at him, and it was like I was seeing things clearly. I was seeing someone who was basically just out for himself. He hadn't loved me. He never would. I'd always be baggage. Me and the baby.

"Look, come back. Finish your coffee. We need to talk. We've got to decide what we're going to do about this."

"But there isn't a 'we', anymore, is there? There's a you and there's a me. Me and the baby. I'll decide what I'm going to do about it."

"What will you do, Lisa?" There was fear in his eyes.

"I'll let you know," I walked away again, and carried on walking. He didn't try to catch me up again. I felt this new energy, firing me. I was alone, I was on my own with this, but I wasn't frightened anymore.

I couldn't see the woman in the grey coat on the platform. She wasn't on the train either, or at least not in my carriage. I was a little disappointed. I wanted to tell her that I had decided what I would do. I wanted her to tell me I had made the right decision. But then as the train started pulling out of the station, I saw her. She was standing right at the end of the platform. She was looking up at me, at my face staring out of the train window, and she was smiling. That lined, tired face, full of life's troubles, seemed to have lifted now.

She looked younger. She looked like me. She lifted a hand and waved to me and I waved back.

That all happened some time ago now. I have a new life now. I'm still working as an aromatherapist, but I've moved. I've moved to a flat near my parents in Ledbury. My mum's retired, so she helps out with Harry when I'm seeing clients. Harry is six months old. He is gorgeous. He is the image of his dad, in looks anyway. I emailed Jack to tell him the baby was born and I sent him a photo. He has been down several times to see Harry and now has decided he does want to be part of his son's life. He has a new girlfriend. I met her once, very briefly, the last time Jack came down to see the baby. She was waiting in the car but I picked up Harry and went outside to say 'Hello'. I was more curious than actually being friendly, but thought it sensible to check her out. She had shoulder length, dark brown hair and a roundish face, like I have. We could've easily been sisters. I don't know if she's another 'casual thing' but if she isn't then maybe she'll be part of Harry's life too, in some way.

It seems to me, that all of us, are like those tiny lights dotting the wire mesh sculptures that Jack and I saw that day at the Tate Modern. There's space between us, yet we are all connected. Apart, and yet together, making something that is more than the sum of our parts.

I haven't got a new boyfriend. I've got Harry, and he's the love of my life, and for now that's enough. I never saw the woman in the grey coat again. I looked for her often. In crowded streets, in shopping malls, on buses and trains. I wanted to show her Harry, to tell her how things had turned out. I wanted to tell her that when I last saw her, that day I met Jack in Euston station, when I said, 'Me and the baby' to him, that was when I decided. I wasn't sure of it till later, but that was the turning point. Because it's very difficult to say the word, baby, and then go and get rid of it. Or at least, that's how it was for me.

As for the woman in the grey coat, I used to think - crazy though it sounds - that she was some sort of future projection of myself. Me in the future. Whether it's the 'me' that had the baby or the 'me' who didn't, I don't know. But then one day I was helping my mum sort through stuff she wanted to throw out. She had these shoeboxes full of old photos from her past and I was sifting through them, looking at all these people, some that I knew and some that I didn't know, and this photo kind of fell out into my lap. Like it wanted itself to be noticed. I picked it up and there's with woman in a grey coat with a face that looks a lot like mine, just older.

'Who's this, mum?"

My mother picked it up and looked at it. "Oh, that. That was your Aunt Susan. Don't you remember me telling you about her? She was my eldest sister, the one who emigrated to America. We didn't see much of her after that. She died of cancer, very shortly after sending me that photo. I think she was ill when that photo was taken. She looks tired in it, older than her years. You were only about twelve when she died. You never met her."

"Something's coming back," I muttered. I did remember, vaguely. I remembered feeling a little sad, briefly, when mum had told me her sister had died. But I never felt the loss of her as an auntie back then when I was growing up. My mother was one of four girls, so there were always other aunties in our life.

'Don't you remember me telling you that she was the one you looked the most like? You're the image of her really, when she was your age."

'Yes, I think so."

I took the photo back and looked at it carefully. Another one of those tiny lights, connected to me for ever, but yet so much space between us that I'd never even met her. Her face could be my face in maybe fifteen or so years' time. It could be me looking sad and tired and disappointed. But yet, somehow I don't think it will be.

"Did she ever have any children, Mum?"

"No, she never did. Although she did write me once, about something that happened. She was much younger. I think there was some man who hadn't treated her that well. Not sure of the details. But I think she was expecting, but then lost the baby. Or maybe got rid of it ......It upset her a lot. Shame you never met her."

"Yes," I said. "It is a shame."

Reptiles
John Simes

Dear reader, while doing the research for my next novel, I took a train journey. You may know it very well....

August had burnished the green meadows into dazzling gold; fields of maize and wheat furrowed and furled as the winds played among the shifting ranks of cornstalks. Peter Young will take this same train journey, I mused, and scribbled some notes on my e-pad; I recall now the secret smile that must have played across my lips in that moment. Peter Young will take this same journey to find himself – as I was. Skuas and sandpipers darted like jets above silent inland ponds and grassy dunes, resplendent with juniper and shimmering mosses of maidenhair and pointed spear. The roly-poly golfers, colourfully retired, waddling across Dawlish Warren, were of passing comic fascination – 'dinosaurs on vacation', I noted. As the train trembled and swayed along the estuary rim, I pondered the message on my e-phone: "Sorry I can't make it, old boy. Prime minister in a tizzy. Gave my ticket to an old friend. He wants to meet you. Enjoy the match."

I always liked to travel on my own – preferring the company of strangers on a journey.   Peter and his girlfriend, Navinda Eman, are the characters from The Dream Factory. Both aged seventeen - you could call it a 'coming-of-age love story'. Peter is like me, idle, only switches on when it suits him. Navinda, from a Palestinian family, determined, focused, formidably intelligent. But I had to 'put Navinda together' as a character – I had never met anyone quite like her. So far. And I was struggling for a theme. For all the unrolling of chapters, and unfurling of landscape and words, it had to be about....well... something!

The train slow-turned and accelerated. I felt the excitement, the momentum of change. Soon I would be drifting anonymously through the Grace Gates at Lords and ascending the steps of the East Clock Tower and take my seat in the Thomas Lord box. The emerald green of the playing area would dazzle, as the players – like alien giants – would perform stretches and hurl cricket balls or jog backwards to take steepling catches. But this time there would be a stranger in the seat next to mine; I pictured a white Panama hat, motionless, above a striped blazer and neat haircut.

Out the window, the waves rolled up the estuary; the train surged beyond them and struck across country, the arteries of rivers and motorways sliding beneath as we traversed bridges and swept along embankments. I shook out my newspaper. The pope's visit to London was coming up – it was across the papers. I snorted. I had no time for movements, clubs, sects, organized religions, and yet, I had to admit, the idea of faith preoccupied me. My journey, I knew, was one of faith but where would it take me? Did it matter? But religious leaders? No way. Count me out.

A student looked up from the essay she'd been writing on the table opposite me. Her cocoa-brown eyes stared at me through her round eyeglasses; a stud shone from her nose, and a tattoo appeared to be sliding its fiery fingers across her shoulder. "Can I look?" she enquired.

"Of course." I slid the newspaper across. She refolded it to display the whole article. Her fingers followed the text and she grunted.

"Stupid old bastard!" she exclaimed. A woman looked up from her novel, and a smart-suited young man next to me lowered his e-pad. She read more. "Yeah, right on." She stood up. "Listen to this, folks." All heads turned to look as the colour drained from my face. "Listen to this! It's cool! 'The pope's opposition to condoms kills people. It is all very well – his lecturing us on morals – but he should look at his

86

own organization. He will be met with the most utter, exquisite, grovelling politeness, and with that, somehow we're in an uncivilized third world country'. Ain't that the truth!"

As the young woman's tirade continued, my body shrunk and shrivelled like a leaf in the fire.

She waved a bangled arm in the air. "Oh, there's more. 'What is civilized about demeaning women, demonizing homosexuals, wishing that IVF children had never been born? Our only crime has been silence." By this time my toes were curling up inside my shoes; a bead of sweat rolled down my brow. This girl stood there, bold and defiant, daring fellow passengers to disagree. A burst of applause came from the seat behind me and was picked up by others farther down the coach. The older woman had shrunk back to her novel. I closed my eyes – This will be over soon, I thought.

"But we must have leaders," the man next to me piped up, prolonging my agony.

The student fixed him in his seat, her hands on her hips in a gesture that reminded me of a Victorian teapot. "Yes, but wouldn't it be nice to have a pope – if we must have one – who isn't totally bloody embarrassing?" He visibly withered under her stare.

She sat down slowly, absorbing the trembling silence that had descended on the passengers. Her eyes found me again. "Do you agree with that?" Her finger jabbed the newspaper once again, before she slid it back across the table. Oh, lord, she's still going, I thought. "Do you?"

Inside me something turned over; I felt naked. "Until just now, I didn't know." I breathed deeply. Best to be honest, but what did I really believe? She continued to stare at me. "I also think we must have leaders…" Her eyes flickered, and her lips began to form a response. "We must have leaders." She raised an eyebrow. "And…I think I've just met one. I'm glad you said what you did."

My hesitancy wasn't because I didn't trust any political group or faith; it was because I didn't have the courage to be wrong. It was fear. I admired this student because she wasn't afraid; she would stare threats in the face. Like Peter. Like Navinda. I felt humbled. "You remind me of two young people I know…" I trailed off, averting my eyes. "Two young friends of mine."

"I would like to meet them," she said.

"Not possible."

"Not possible?"

"No."

"Why?"

I shook my head. "Hard to explain." I looked away.

The student resumed her essay, scribbling rapidly and periodically flipping the pages of her notepad. She seized her e-phone and scrolled through her messages. "You realize we won't meet again." She looked at me quizzically. "What are the odds of that happening?"

I pondered briefly. "Seven million to one?"

She smiled. "More than that. More than when we got on this train."

"I'll let you do the maths."

"The thing is," she continued, fixing me once again with her eyes, "I believe you have to seize the moment. You must speak up. Not to say anything is a crime. Don't you agree?" She placed her eyeglasses on the table and removed a clasp from the back of her head; her dark hair tumbled about her shoulders. Who is this girl? Do I know her? I knew I did, but I couldn't explain how. "I'm sorry if I embarrassed you."

I shook my head. "I wasn't embarrassed."

"You were." She chuckled. "I could tell."

"No." But I was feeling embarrassed now.

"You went red. Then you looked out the window."

I smiled. "You found me out." I was praying I wouldn't blush again.

The train slid into London's Paddington station, the curved platforms slipping like fingers on either side of the train. She stood up and pulled down her rucksack, shoving her notepad and book into the pack. Then she unzipped a side pocket for her e-phone.

The train halted. I stood up and retrieved my newspaper and bag. I extended my hand. "Goodbye." The girl smiled and shook my hand. I felt her cool, slender fingers in my palm and shivered.

"Goodbye," she said. "Talking is good. Without it, there is no truth. Nothing changes." Was this happening to me? The hairs on the back of my neck rose. "Don't you agree?" She drew the straps of her pack across her shoulders and joined the passenger queue shuffling down the train. I just stood there, gaping and foolish. The queue shuffled forward; she looked back fleetingly and smiled. I glanced down at the table. There was scrap of paper. She had written, "The man who never alters his opinions is like standing water, and breeds reptiles of the mind."

"You all right, chief?"

I turned. The carriage was empty. The student had gone, but she had left me with the precious gift of a theme. The ticket collector stood in his grey uniform, his glasses glinting above a broad smile. "The train terminates 'ere, Guv."

Zlata
Christine Genovese

Or

A Prequel to Tchaikovsky's 1812 Overture and its Grandiose Finale.

Tashya Romanovich, wife of Fyodor Romanovich.

Most of that month of June was glorious. The general store of our ever resourceful Dmitri spilled out into the road with benches and tables where we gathered during those long, balmy evenings. The kvass flowed freely and the piroshky were delicious. We had plenty to celebrate. The hay had been brought in and stored away. It was a good harvest; our cattle would be well fed during the winter months. The potatoes were at their early-season best and we had a glut of broad beans. Old Piotr often came along with his fiddle and when he played a polka Fyodor and I danced. Others joined in and the rest picked up the rhythm, clapping their hands and stamping their feet, faster and faster till neither dancers nor fiddler could keep up.

You could almost hear the village humming with contentment. My own happiness soared above all this. I was newly wed to Fyodor and I wore a blissful grin for all to see. We shared our plentiful blessings inside our soft cocoon of love. We had some chickens as well as Zlata, our pig. We tended a small field of turnips and some vegetables for our own table. Nina and Dina, our two huskies, were Fyodor's companions when he went hunting. The three of them happily accepted me as part of the team, especially when they realised I still possessed the hunting skills my father had taught me from an early age. I considered myself lucky I didn't have a brother for my father to favour.

June was nearly over when the first rumours – constant, uneasy rumblings – reached our village and caused a stir outside Dmitri's store. We thought some of the earliest accounts were wild fabrications, stories still floating in the air from the time when our Babushka gathered us children together. We used to sit at her feet, huddled on fur rugs, holding our breaths and wide-eyed with frightened excitement when she told us how the evil witch, Baba Yaga, killed, cooked and ate innocent children and cackled with delight when destruction and brutality reigned supreme. Babushka never forgot to remind us that Baba Yaga had been chased far away into the mountains where she could do no harm.

Now it seemed she had returned. We tried not to believe it until our own locals confirmed sightings of Napoleon's army, 'La Grande Armée', marching east towards Moscow. They swore they'd seen an endless column of soldiers, as wide as a river and extending further than the eye could reach, all marching in time and ready to set up their cannons and fire at attackers at a moment's notice. They had more horses than the Cossacks; some were cavalry horses while others were strong cobs drawing vehicles with artillery and other supplies. Indeed, it was said they'd brought their own luxury food and wine which they served with silver cutlery and crystal glasses. Some officers were accompanied by their wives and children as if for a holiday. But as they advanced, they killed, raped and pillaged whatever lay in the way of their progress.

Few thought the Tsar's army could drive this invader out of our country. We waited anxiously for news. Then we learnt that, instead of attacking, our forces burnt down every town and village along the route of the advancing enemy. There were battles and skirmishes but nothing that brought the situation any nearer to a conclusion. We heard that La Grande Armée was running out of fodder for their horses. Their other supplies were low as well. We were shocked when news came that Moscow, too, had been torched. The Tsar sent no envoys to Moscow to negotiate a peace – and certainly not to surrender.

The summer was peaceful enough in our village once the shock of La Grande Armée marching past faded into a vague fear for parts of the country that we knew little about. We tended our crops and our animals and Fyodor and I were too wrapped up in the wonderful adventure of our love to let faraway problems cast a shadow over it. We often went fishing in the Berezina River or we hunted for wolves and foxes and traded furs in the usual way.

Zlata, our pig, became skitty and restless towards the end of July. When we let her into the enclosure where Razumikhin kept his magnificent boar the reason became obvious, and after the two of them had spent an enjoyable amorous afternoon together, Zlata returned calmly to her own pen with a new, philosophical glint in her eyes. Fyodor caught me in his arms and swung me up in the air. "Tashya, my love," he laughed, "I think Zlata is trying to beat us to it!"

The French troops stayed in Moscow until the middle of October. We heard there was disorder amongst the men as hunger and diseases ravaged their ranks. Then winter set in. We'd never seen a winter like that in October with fierce snowstorms and temperatures that dropped way below what was normal for January. The Berezina froze over so that we couldn't go fishing there. We harvested what we could before the ground froze and placed winter stores in the barns. Fyodor and I built a lean-to shed against the chimney wall of our cottage. That should keep Zlata warm enough for when her time came to farrow. We got our skis, the sleigh and the harnesses ready for hunting trips while Nina and Dina danced around us in excited circles. They were eager to go off on their favourite employment and our trial sleigh trip on the frozen river was an almost delirious thrill for the four of us.

La Grande Armée packed up and started their lengthy retreat through the snow from Moscow. Soldiers and horses dropped by the roadside as freezing temperatures, illness and injuries hampered their progress. It was as if they were haunted by ill-luck, or, as Babushka would have said: the Kikimora had joined their ranks and everything they undertook from that moment would turn to disaster. The Kikimora could make you kill your best friend and eat him, if it wanted to. Once it's got a foothold in your existence the Kikimora never lets go.

When the ragged remains of La Grande Armée approached our area we received a visit from our government officials who told us to leave our village as it was going to be torched. This was in mid-November and they gave us a week's warning and suggested that we went to a village north-east of ours where we'd be safe and welcomed by the locals.

We had not expected this. The blow left our village in shock. There was no argument about it. It was better to burn our village than to have it ransacked and destroyed by brutal foreigners. The wintry storm howled in sympathy for us, making it harder to pack a few belongings into carts for the village's five horses to draw. All other animals were to be slaughtered to avoid them dying a cruel death by fire.

There was keening in the air from several cottages. Some thought they heard a darker, more vicious, rattling howl in the depths of the thick freezing gale. I knew what that meant, and what happened next confirmed my worst fears. The Kikimora had acquired immense powers from preying on the disintegrating French army. It was now coming our way with increased fury.

We continued packing the carts. I explained a plan I'd been hatching to the other villagers. What if we drove the animals up into the woods where there was a small clearing? We could use ropes for a makeshift enclosure and come back for them when the danger was over.

It was Gorovsky who'd received the government delegation at his house, and when nobody else said anything, he felt he had to speak up. "Tashya," he said, "what you're proposing is very tempting because of our attachment to our animals. They're our livelihood and we do not want them to die. The fact is, however, that we've received clear orders from the official delegation and disobeying those orders would be treason."

Nothing else was said on the matter and when darkness fell we retired to our separate homes. I was alone that night as Fyodor had been requisitioned to join an army squadron and help them select places where lines of sharp pickets hammered into the ground would slow down the French army's progress and perhaps trip up and injure their exhausted horses. Nobody knew the lay of the land better than Fyodor and he'd gone as their guide with the sleigh and the dogs. They'd warned me they might need him to bivouac with them for the night, so I wasn't unduly worried.

As I tried to while away the time I noticed that there was more traffic than usual between the houses. When we met at daybreak the following morning to continue our work I found out that they'd been discussing my plan for sparing the animals. After much weighing up of the pros and the cons they'd come to the conclusion that it was better for everyone to avoid the mass slaughter of our cattle and they were ready to set up the temporary enclosure. I was so relieved I could have hugged them all. Zlata was foremost in my mind, I admit, as her time was getting close. The gestation period is three months, three weeks and three days, they say, which would make it one of the last days in November. After all, wars aren't fought by animals, and why should ours be casualties of a war that didn't concern them?

When dusk started to blur the horizon we were surprised by the arrival of panting, frantic dogs pulling an empty sleigh into the village. My legs gave way and I sank into the snow. I felt a spasm of grief inside me. I wondered whether that was our child that grieved for a lost father, or died of that sudden grief, or sighed in despair because it would never be born. Neighbours picked me up and took me home where they tucked me in on the bed and tried to reassure me that we didn't know for sure what had happened. But I knew. Nina and Dina knew. They wouldn't have returned without him otherwise.

There was a slight thaw the next few days. I went with the villagers and our animals up the hill and into the woods where we roped in a clearing. I looked into Zlata's eyes when we parted and made her a solemn promise that I'd be with her when she farrowed. I told her she would be the best mother ever for her many piglets. She would raise them till they were ready to have litters of their own and she would become a wonderful Babushka. I tied my own wishes up with Zlata's, creating a sacred bond between us.

I wasn't much help during the final days of our village. My mind folded in on itself and switched off from my surroundings. I didn't even realise when tears were running down my cheeks until someone put an arm round me with an offer of sympathy.

The area was crawling with dangers that as yet weren't much more than a feeling that no one was safe. Spies, scouts and stray groups of enemy soldiers were sometimes seen, and we feared their threatening presence everywhere. Everyone was jumpy. The slightest noise or movement might reveal a deathly danger. But when little Stanislav, the shepherd boy, came sprinting down from the woods, we froze with apprehension.

Stanislav had been on his way up to check on our cattle. When he heard some men speaking in a rough foreign language he hid behind a tree. There was nothing he could do and he just stood there, helplessly watching the ragged soldiers using the enclosure ropes to tie up the animals and lead them off in the direction of their encampment.

I thought I heard the Kikimora roaring with laughter. Zlata had been taken away. I'd given my promise to Zlata.

Our villagers left at dawn the following morning. An army squadron was due to arrive towards evening to burn our homes and our crops to the ground.

I told them I'd catch up with them later. I told them I'd just remembered some traps Fyodor had set up and I needed to check and remove them. I told them I wouldn't be long. That's what I told them.

Laurent Duclos, farrier at the 14th French Cavalry Regiment.

Some think the instinct for survival is a noble sentiment. They're wrong. It is worse than ignoble; it is the most debasing, the most ignominious urge that can possess a person.

What do you call someone who kills his friend to steal his overcoat? Who walks past those dying in the snow without a glance? Who's driven to eat human flesh?

The instinct for survival changes men into monsters.

We started this campaign with 100,000 magnificent horses. I was a farrier and horse doctor and proud of my post.

My father is the blacksmith of our small village in the French Alps. When I was conscripted into the army he said it was like losing his youthful strength in one blow. Without me there was only a sad, old man left to run the smithy, he said … with more emotion than was usual for him.

I'd spent my childhood in the forge whenever I was allowed in. We'd invented a special family ritual around the time when I turned five. On my birthday I was invited to stand in my father's work place and attempt to lift up the heavy hammer and deliver a blow to the anvil. My mother and sister stood watching, urging me on and commenting on my growing strength as the years went by. My father had promised me that as soon as I was strong enough to swing the hammer he'd take me on as his apprentice.

In the meantime the Revolution ran its long and sometimes gruesome course. News of all sorts reached us regularly in our Alpine village and my parents shook their heads and wondered what would become of our nation. The events, however, happened far away and didn't affect our village to a great extent. The local baron lost his title and his lands. He kept his herd of cows and the pasture, and his cowherds, milkmaids and dairymen continued to work for him in the usual way.

The dissolution of a nearby monastery brought one of the monks back to our village where he was born. The old schoolmaster welcomed the opportunity to retire, leaving Brother Bernard – no longer a Brother – in charge of the village school. His unusual teaching methods tricked our class of about 16 boys and girls into learning the three R's for the fun of it.

When we'd done our lessons to Brother Bernard's satisfaction he often treated us to a story. That was one of the reasons we worked so hard; he knew how to tell a story. My favourites were about King Arthur and his Knights – and one story in particular. I never tired of hearing how the young Arthur's princely strength grew and grew until one day he gripped the famous Excalibur sword and swung it free from the stone where it was trapped.

I achieved my Excalibur feat on my 14th birthday – the happiest day in my life. I revelled in the admiration and applause of my family as I heaved the hammer high up above my head and brought it down on the anvil with a clang that rang out more melodiously to my ears than if it were the music of the spheres … my pride was more than a match for Arthur's.

I was good with horses and everything that involved horses. Now I learnt to master how to shoe a horse. I also wanted to treat their common ailments and I discovered that my former teacher, Brother Bernard, was a skilled medical man. He taught me to use the local eau-de-vie to prevent wounds from festering. He also explained the virtues of some plants and showed me how to prepare and administer them in specific cases. I gradually became the proud owner of a well-stocked pharmacy set up with Brother Bernard's help. We collected common herbs and plants like dandelion and vervain for parasites; sorrel and yarrow for fevers, willow bark for pain and much more. My skills became known and appreciated, and my love of horses grew with my knowledge of how to care for them. The recruitment officer knew of my reputation in this field and enrolled me as farrier in the cavalry.

Horses are gentle and patient creatures. They'll put up with a lot from the owner they trust. They're powerful and can charge through enemy lines while their riders cut down everything in their way. There's a protective complicity between horse and rider. They rely on one another for survival. But unlike men, horses are neither brave nor aggressive by nature. A fatally injured horse is panic-stricken when faced with death. A soldier must never look a dying horse in the eyes. He'd be looking into the bottomless, black pit of animal misery. He'd see the despair of a creature whose belief in goodness is shattered as it discovers the treacherous deception and the pointlessness and absurdity of so many wasted lives.

That was the condition of those horses and men who were left to undertake the strenuous retreat from Moscow.

There was no water and no fodder for the horses. They weren't shod for the frozen terrain. They stumbled and broke their legs. I, the horse doctor, became horse butcher when their strength failed.

Tashya would never treat animals that way.

I caught sight of her near the animal enclosure on the edge of our encampment on the night before we were to cross the Berezina River. She did a low whistle and the sow twitched her ears and trundled over to the improvised barrier. When she'd cut the rope the sow followed her into the dark. I noticed the sow's heavy waddle. It stopped me short. The sow was in pig.

I had a delirious flash of our hunger-crazed soldiers ripping the sow open; of their uncomprehending grins as purple foetuses and blood spilt out in the snow; of how they'd spear them on their bayonets … I retched.

It was as if an axe split me down the middle. The soldier part fell away like a gangrenous limb. I put on my skis to follow the woman and her sow.

I caught up with her at the sleigh. She turned on me with a hunting knife, ready to defend her charge. I gestured my intentions and she accepted in a matter-of-fact way. We secured Zlata on the sleigh and skied off into the forest till we reached a small stone-built hunting shelter.

She had equipped it well: straw bedding, firewood, a mound of turnips, some hay-bales.

Tashya got the fire going and we watched Zlata pushing the straw around. She took her time but eventually she slumped down in her prepared nest and started breathing noisily. Tashya stroked her snout and whispered comforting words. What followed was as magical as the sprouting of spring flowers and the songs of skylarks in my Alpine homeland.

Zlata grunted and groaned to the rhythm of her contractions. Tashya shouted encouragement and I whooped in delight every time a slippery little wriggling piglet popped out with a surprised squeal. I helped every one of them out and presented Zlata with her beautiful offspring. She snuffled them and bit off the umbilical cord and nuzzled them off in the direction of her teats where they instantly clamped on. After the tenth piglet there was a pause and we thought she'd finished. The eleventh piglet needed a helping hand and I plunged my hand into the birth canal to check. I caught the twelfth piglet by a hind leg and gently eased it out under protest from both mother and baby.

When the twelve healthy piglets were suckling from Zlata's swollen dugs I held my arms out to Tashya and we hugged and did a mad dance round the room. Nina and Dina were allowed in and warned by Tashya's command and Zlata's grunts to welcome the family additions with respect. They sniffed and licked and settled by the fire.

We kept a constant vigil to make sure Zlata didn't accidentally crush one of her piglets. They soon learnt to watch out for themselves and we tended to other tasks. Tashya went hunting and fishing to supplement our daily diet of turnips, and I went into the forest for firewood.

I'd admired Tashya from the moment I observed her courage in stealing Zlata away from right under our noses. It wasn't long before I realised that I was falling in love with her, and I was sad when she brushed off even my most timid advance. She slept in her corner with Nina and Dina by her side, and I knew better than to try to disturb her. We lived like two lost children in a fairytale who've found an enchanted cottage deep in the forest where no evil forces could reach us.

Tashya was a skilled hunter but sometimes a snowstorm made conditions too hazardous and she'd come back empty-handed. We ate turnips. And more turnips. This happened several days in a row while I'd spent endless hours in bad weather lugging a large tree-trunk back from the forest and splitting it into logs. Hunger and exhaustion tormented me when I carried the final armload of firewood into the hut where Tashya was tending the animals. I flung the firewood down. Turnips simmered in the pot – bland and insufficient – mocking me, provoking me.

Soldiers do not question their actions. Soldiers act. With hunger-crazed military resoluteness I seized a piglet by the hind-legs. Then I looked around for the knife.

"Nyet!" The word hit me like the crack of a whip. She stood there, flanked by the dogs. I stared into three almost identical pairs of icy-blue, court-martial eyes.

I sank to my knees, I blabbered. She pointed to the door. The dogs growled. They frog-marched me out. I put on my skis and sped off into the night.

Tashya.

I cried that night. I howled and sobbed and beat the walls of the hut with my fists. It wasn't so much because Laurent had gone. It wasn't my grief over Fyodor's death either. It was about how and why my life and the world around me had been robbed of so much happiness.

Laurent could have shot me when he discovered me near their encampment. Or worse: he could have captured me and let the soldiers use me as a plaything before killing me. He did neither. He made a choice between two options; the first was the death and destruction of war. That was the side he was contracted to, whether he liked it or not. The second was to join me in the life-giving care of Zlata; that would brand him as a deserter. But that was the option he chose. I deserted my fellow villagers for the same reason when they left everything behind them.

Like all good hunters, including my father, Fyodor had a deep reverence for fertility. He knew the breeding habits of all the animals, from the smallest songbird to the biggest bear. He never hunted an animal during its breeding season. It was to ensure a plentiful supply for the future, he explained. When Zlata became pregnant he spoilt her. He was waiting to spoil me when my fertility showed itself.

But the war killed Fyodor. The war also left a festering wound in Laurent's soul: the urge to survive at all costs. Or did the Kikimora do it? Perhaps the Kikimora had merged with the war into one all-powerful evil spirit that no amount of juniper branches could ward off.

Had the curse crept into my heart as well? It wasn't Laurent's fault that his army killed Fyodor. Laurent renounced the war, and his help and care made our existence in this hut a happy one. Except for that one thing. Yet I loved him dearly. He was kind, gentle and attractive. Would he have resisted the urge to kill if I hadn't rejected him? The question troubled me. I'd kept my promise to Zlata. I'd saved one of her piglets from death and would continue to protect the rest. Perhaps the hidden part of our pact would come true as well.

My tearful outburst that night had exhausted me both physically and emotionally. It was the first time since Fyodor's death that I'd given free vent to my grief. I noticed that Zlata and her piglets were unusually quiet while Dina and Nina sat huddled together and panting in a corner of the hut. I felt sorry that I'd caused them anxiety by my excessive behaviour. I knelt down and gave the dogs a loving cuddle and their closeness soothed me. The slurping suckling noises from Zlata's piglets resumed and I nearly burst into a giggle as I realised that my animal family had forgiven me. A faint flutter of something new and fragile inside me lifted my spirits. I'd had several of these lately, but this one was unmistakably from the life I was carrying in my womb. I was nearly halfway through, I thought. The winter would be long and hard, but we'd survive.

Can I Count on Your Support?
Gwynneth Chubb

I opened the door. There he stood, sharp suit, tie in party colours, sincere smile fixed in place.

"Good morning," he chirped. "I'd like to talk to you about our plans to make your life better." He pivoted towards the gate in expectation of a refusal.

'Talk away,' I said.

"Oh! Gosh!" he said trotting back from the garden gate. "Well, I'd like to start with what we're going to do for hard-working families like yours."

'Well,' I said, 'It depends on your definition of a hard-working family.'

"The usual," he said, "Mum and Dad working hard and two point four children."

'Hmm. What about Mum and Dad working hard and being paid nowt? What about Mum and Mum or Dad and Dad? What about just Mum or just Dad. What about people without children? Look at us. We did have exactly 2.4 children at one time. You might think that impossible but I lost the twin of my youngest at 16 weeks so he was exactly point four, you see.'

The man winced. I carried on.

'Our kids left home long ago so there's just the two of us. Could you call us hard-working? I get up at nine-ish each morning, have my breakfast, spend some time reading the paper that my partner has fetched, have a desultory coffee, then it's time for lunch, something easy like a soup or a sandwich. If it's really hot like this, I then lie down in the conservatory, shut my eyes and imagine I'm in the Mediterranean while I have a nap. Hubby makes the dinner, then I might stay in or go out to one of my activities. Do you count that as hard-working?'

"I'm sure you've worked hard all your life. You deserve to relax now in your old age."

'But I thought you said we're all in this together!"

"Yes, of course we are. You're a poor pensioner and we're going to make sure that you keep your bus passes and your winter fuel allowance. We won't let austerity grind you down. Don't you worry, my dear."

'I'm not worrying, thank you. We're better off than when we were working! I don't need fuel allowances. Why can't we opt out so that the government can give it to those who really do need it? If there were no bus passes, I'd just go to town in the car."

'Look, all I can say is that we're working to a big plan to make life better for everyone. What do you think about all these immigrants coming here?"

'Ooh, Isn't it marvellous! What would we do without them? Our NHS would collapse, there'd be no workers in McDonald's - wonderful place that for a cheap meal. You should try it, dear. You look a bit undernourished, if you don't mind me saying so. I love my food. We're so lucky here. We have food from all over the world. Just go down to the market and have a look. I'm so glad you're not one of those dreadful people who go on about immigrants wrecking our country.'

"Well, they do stop our own people getting jobs you know."

'But you're going to spend lots of money on education for our own youngsters, aren't you, to get them up to the same level as these wonderful East Europeans?'

"Of course, we're going to spend money on education.

How can we do that if we stay in Europe?"

'It's the right thing to do, isn't it, dear. Spend money on education so that our young people are qualified to do all these jobs. Then we won't need to rob poor old Poland of their skilled electricians, the Philippines and other developing countries of the qualified doctors and nurses that they must need so desperately for themselves. It's not right that we take these people away from their families whilst our young are thrown onto the streets or in dead-end jobs, is it, dear? I'm so glad you can see that too. Not many politicians can these days.'

He smiled at the compliment, then put on a stern expression. "We have to pay down the deficit in order to be able to afford to spend."

'Quite right too. It's about time the rich paid their way. What does it say in that manifesto about stopping tax avoidance?'

He searched for the right page. "Er… it says we're looking at stopping benefit scroungers."

'Yes, that'll raise a tiny bit. Do you know any, dear? They seem awfully hard to find when you want one.'

"Housing, we must build more houses."

'Who for, dear? All the ones round here cost nearly half a million. I expect you're going to raise stamp duty to enormous levels on those houses to get enough money to build council houses, aren't you? That's a brilliant idea. Glad to see you're thinking these issues through. After all, we hard-working families are all in this together in doing the right thing, aren't we?'

A confused look flashed across his face as Party Man took his leave and headed for the garden gate once more.

Photo intro
Dave Hutton

Following on from the last Arts Quarter Books publication, 'Arts and Minds', it has been my privilege again to take photographs of artists at work in their studios. I like to capture the environment within which the creative process occurs. This time, I have been helped by fellow local photographers. The artists are all working in Devon.

I would like to thank the artists involved for their participation in this project, and Tejas Earp, Ken Holland and Nigel West for their photos. See the Biographies Section at the back of the book for further information about the artists featured.

Christopher Pitman © Nigel West

Christine Dodd © Dave Hutton

Frank Phillips © Dave Hutton

Emma Childs © Tejas Earp

Mark Jessett © Dave Hutton

Nicholas Eastwood © Ken Holland

Barbara Chavasse © Dave Hutton

Trevor Meadows © Dave Hutton

Ruth Moorey © Dave Hutton

Jayne Farleigh © Dave Hutton

Unresolved Mind
Tejas Earp

A buried heart resurrected
A moment of nostalgia
A memory triggered
By a photograph

The dark days melted away
Evenings spent enjoying the Moonlight
Destiny interferes
Heartaches

Passionate memories
When only two people existed
Entwined within themselves
Souls on fire
Stinging with desire

Within a dream
Reckless Fate
Collided
Shattering precious Dreams

Aromas of India
Tejas Earp

Taking that first step out
A hot blast of warm humid air
Ignites the nostrils
Fragrant incense, pungent spices

Taking another step out
A cornucopia of activity
Hot perspiring body odour
Stale and musty

Take a step sideways
There are cows
Ambling side by side
Mingling with treacherous traffic
Acrid fumes, stench of decay.

Taking a step forwards
Technology vies with traditions
Wealth conflicting with poverty
Agitation in the air
Everyone for themselves

Taking a step backwards
Mughals, East India Company,
Raj, Gandhi, Nehru echoing
Stagnant essence of
Upheavals in History regurgitated

Disappearances - Five Poems
Robin Barton

A Summer Evening on the Heath

A summer evening on the heath:
trees at its edge lose detail, become silhouettes,
become
Van Gogh's pine tree in his starry night.

The sky is a pale blue-grey;
down in the plain across islands of fir and pine and away to
the far horizon's edge
the sky is slowly smothering
a last faint gash
of gold.

The lane slopes away into
a tunnel of darkness,
the evening settles to its mothy shadows,
insects faintly prick the silence;
to them the next sound may strike fear:
a faint churring begins;
you have to stop, turn your head, turn it again — the sound
cannot be
fixed to a spot:
the range-finder in your ears has malfunctioned, there must
be
more than one source,
more than six —
no, after all it is one.

But some ventriloquist is making it.

A sudden buzz —
a clumsy near miss close to your ear:
a heavy moth,

the air expresses bat shapes which are no more
than disappearances.

The churring is a permanent soundscape.

Now there are snaps in the air—
boomerang wings clap and pause, clap and pause,
the night bird swings and floats, swings and floats.
The churring has layers: if one layer disappears another,
nearer or more distant
takes its place.

Moths and beetles beware: here among bats and owls,
erratically cruises
the nightjar.

At the Wood's Edge

At the edge of the wood I sit in the sun,

Above me tall pines and thickets of thorn.

Below, a field slopes and shadows pass

As cloud and sunlight softly contend

When summer grips spring in a strong embrace.

Across the valley another wood

Where alder and larch and whitebeam stand,

Where wrens in ivy trill at their nests

Where once, sadly addled, some eggs we found

And the owl pierced the night with his ghostly cry.

With the wood at my back I am walled and secure,

For behind the wood is a sunken lane

And another wood and another field

And the quiet river silverly glides

And peace is the noontide blessing on all.

No quieter spot lives under the sun,

Though a rustle of winter leaves may stir,

While I turn my page or lift my gaze

To wonder at lives of smallest scope

The ant, the beetle, the bee in its flower,

The swallow, the moth or the tortoiseshell.

Yet here there are ghosts of darker days

And at the wood's corner, now smothered, scarce seen,

A rotting hut, broken and tangled with brier,

Within, a piano, worm-eaten and warped

But only harsh janglings you still might evoke:

For next to the hut, smashed and sunken in earth

A circle of steel and glass smithereens

Are all that remain of the thunder of war —

A searchlight's black skeleton, once a brave eye

To blazon an enemy high in the night;

And echoes of that time so distant, yet here,

A faint obbligato of fear-filled days

To counterpoint peace and these sun-filled hours,

And now only cloud shadows, passing like these.

Tipping Point – *Almost a Sonnet*

The morning stretches grey up to the moor,

Down the long valley lies a tongue of mist.

In alders, brambles, or in tamarisk,

Against the light, stencilled in sycamore

A linnet sweetly pricks the air with song.

From far across the bay the dawning grows,

Pines scent the air, an early golfer strolls,

A skylark trills, a jogger swings along,

Beside his path the black slugs slickly shine.

A stonechat   chafes the air to warn his mate

A buzzard soars and yelps and sees a sign –

A beetle stirring, heedless of its fate.

But on this God-gift turf in harsh antithesis

Lie prams, beds, tires and trash: this is

– a tipping point.

Trapped

Within dim misted lights and giant trees,

Within intimidating heat, breathless humidity,

The fatal exudations sweat down trunks

Riven by gnarled old age, a billion years ago.

Around some smooth alluring necks today

We see the golden moments time has wrought

When, resting fatally, some fly or moth,

Some busy ant, some mantis, wasp or bug

Some millipede or nectar laden bee,

With but a careless touch was mired and trapped

And knew its slow inevitable fate.

Like lava creeping and enveloping

Stifling all efforts, feeble helplessness,

The amber from the ancient pine crept down

And drowned its victims hour by silent hour

That now the creatures' direst agonies

As cruel gifts of time adorn and charm.

Disguises

Out on the sea white triangles,
Mere pictures on a calm expanse.
Distance removes whatever life
Could be unveiled by nearer view.

An old man's gnarled and rheumy face.
Saddens the street he rides along
But years ago he changed the world
With courage in war's crucible.

Upon an arid desert floor
Where fires have left black-silvered ash
With bark-like black-leaved deadly skin
A lizard, glue-tongued, swallows ants.

A tiger burns in dappled light:
All unaware a fawn might dream
Of mother's milk, until a paw
Or nightmare fang secures its end.

A squalid caterpillar squirms

Or with snake eyes repels its foes

But sheds its skin and wakens wings

To jewel gardens' summer days.

Do all things wear a lying mask

And hide within a secret sin –

Or triumph – that the world knows not,

Or nurture beauty with disguise?

Birds of a Feather
Liz Green

A bird, blown in on westerlies. Birdwatchers, flown in by helicopter.

Yesterday's storm left a chaos of branches and a lingering chill comfortless as a sodden blanket. And a bird. An accidental, they call them. News fluttered along the avian grapevine and columns of twitchers descended, warlike, on this tiny neck of land, their foreheads speckled with beads of excitement and quiet desperation.

The capricious bird darts and flits.

'There it is.'

'What, that plain thing?'

'No, that's just a sparrow.'

'Over there!'

A collective sigh of relief for there it is, the yellow-breasted bunting with its black face and eponymous yellow breast. It trills, self-important, then skips over a hedge. Bodies surge, a riot of arms and legs and clattering tripods in pursuit of their quarry. They see a departing tail.

*****

A starlet. Her fans. Yards - worlds - away.

The long lenses of the paparazzi, waiting to shoot. A clamouring of well-wishers and the merely curious, their tiny cameras ready to snap.

'There she is.'

'She looks so ordinary.'

'Oh, no, that's her assistant.'

'Over there!'

They exhale. She is there, walking tall. voice tinkling. She carries a fluffy dog, diamante collar sparkling, in a pink bag. As she puts the bag down the dog's attention is caught by a movement, a stirring of leaves in the bushes. It slips its lead.

*****

A dog, holding something in its mouth. All that is visible is a yellow breast. The best view anybody's had all day.

Of Age
Olive Mackintosh-Lowe

Amarnah stood at the entrance to Bond Street Station with her phone in her hand. The day had been warm but now rain speckled the pavement slabs and a sweaty fug rose from the crowd. Shoppers and business people streamed past, jostling her small frame. She shifted the backpack at her feet closer to her. Felt soothed by the weight of the books inside resting against her leg. She checked the time: 20:17. She should have heard from them by now. She tapped out a message to Jude.

How is it going? Xx

She watched the screen for the telltale trail of dots that would let her know he was writing back, that they were done with the doctor. Nothing. She should have gone home on the tube earlier. Been back before they even left. But now she lingered on the street, unwilling to go underground before she'd heard the results.

The buzz of her phone sent a nauseous wave through her body. Adrenalin slicked her wrists and ankles. Her heart beat too close to the surface.

'Hey' She answered. 'You guys done now?'

'Yeah.' Her brother's voice was low, calm. 'It's um… it's not good.'

'No?' Her throat tightened.

'No.'

'Um okay.' she closed her eyes. 'Right I'll come home now. Where are you? You back?'

'No. Pub…mum wants a drink. We are getting a drink then

135

home.'

'Right. I'll be home in like forty minutes okay?'

'Yeah'

'Well done, Jude. Well done for going in with her.'

Her brother didn't say anything. Amarnah could hear her mum in the background, Jude mumbling something back to her.

'Got to go.' He said and the line went quiet.

Amarnah stayed where she stood, unable to think, to move. A big blonde guy in a shiny suit slammed into her right side.

'Sorry' she called after him automatically. He gave her an angry look over his shoulder but kept going. She lifted the heavy bag onto her back and, moving as if she were in a dream, wandered into the station.

She reached the bottom of the escalator and turned into the small supermarket shop. Its refrigerated shelves were scattered with unwanted sandwiches. Single portions of chocolate mousse and rice pudding were encased in expensive-looking packages. Amarnah hung over the selection of flowers for a moment. Didn't lilies use to mean death? Or maybe that was just white flowers in general? Mum liked tulips but that didn't seem right either. The bunch was too small. Their lolling heads seemed flimsy and the clutch of stems felt insubstantial. She picked up a weighty bouquet of yellow roses and headed toward the counter.

'A bottle of brandy, please.' She gestured toward the shelves behind the cashier.

His fat, flushed face twitched into a smug smile. The man

leaned both palms against the counter, chest puffed out.

'I'll have to see your ID'

She rummaged in the top pocket of her rucksack and handed over her driver's license. She felt drained by the action.

'You're too young to be a brandy drinker.' The cashier chuckled. 'Even if you are of age.'

'It's not for me. It's for my mum. She… She' tears stung her eyes. 'She's having a bad day.'

'Yeah?' the cashier's face had fallen.

'Yeah.' Amarnah wiped her eyes on the back of her hand. Took a sharp breath in through her nose. 'How much do I owe you?'

The Texas Yippie
Paula Puolakka

"Today, scorching 102." The teenager in his light-blue and white chequered shirt and Levi's jeans put his pocket radio on the bench and the radio announcer continued with the news. The green grass of the central park, the three-hundred-year-old white oaks, hackberries, and maples, as well as the seven-story redbrick office building, were under the cloudless sky. The children were eating ice cream or playing in the pool of water that was around the fountain.

Roger Miller's "I Know Who It Is" started playing on the radio as the man in the sharp brown suit and black leather shoes stepped inside the café. It was the first song he heard after spending a month in his cabin and away from his obligations at the university and from so-called civilization.

The professor bought a Coke and observed how the Plymouths, Pontiacs, and Fords wormed pass the Nature Bureau. The man behind the counter was about to light a candle that was sticking up from the chocolate cake (that was going to the table where a mother and a father were sitting with their three sons) but managed to snap the matchstick in half. The professor took his lighter and offered fire. The moment the candle grabbed the flame a sudden explosion and a gulping fireball turned the office house and the street next to it into Hell's inferno.

The people in the café screamed and took cover but the professor drank up the Coke to freeze his gut. Finally, when the first wave of shock was gone, and the customers took off to the scene, the professor threw his jacket on his shoulder, a coin on the counter and went in the opposite direction. In his mind, he was praised by the spirits of the ancient mountain trees that the electric company had cut down three weeks earlier and the Nature officials had refused to save.

Devon Limericks
Jill Harrison

There was a young maid from Kingsteignton
Who wished she was living in Peignton.
At quarter to two she could visit the zoo
Before teeing off, up at Deignton.

There was an old man from Totnes
Who lived in a terrible mes
In order to eat he begged on the streat
But nobody knew his addres.

A young man once climbed up Hay Tor
Then crashed down and fractured his jor
And his arm and his neck but he thought 'what the heck?
'Tis a great way to get off the mor.

There was an old man from Torquay
Who fancied a nice cup of tuay
He filled up the pot with water so hot
He scalded his arm and his knuay

There was a young maiden of Honiton
Who struggled to get her new boniton
When draped round her face and secured with pink lace
It made her look quite cosmopoliton

There was a young lady from Ottery
Who made lots of jugs in her pottery
Her kiln was so loaded it almost exploded
Which made her feel faint and quite tottery.

There was a young man of Oakhampton
Who moved his whole family to Bampton
As they wouldn't stop moaning, old friends they kept phoaning
He transferred them all to Northampton

There is a big fish in the Teign
Who seldom, if ever, is seign
On his way to the sea he grabs a cream tea
That wily old pike of the Teign

A gentleman living in Shaldon
Went for a walk up on Haldon
The heather and gorse on the nearby golf corse
Tripped him and caused him to faldon.

There once was a young man from Croyde

Who longed to be aptly employed

He knocked on all doors even begged from all foors

That penniless fellow from Croyde

Restless Characters
Wendy Swarbrick

I love my shop. Tucked between a café and a curio store, it's an old building of nooks and crannies. There are shelves slotted into every niche, with books, new and second-hand, crammed into each space. Organised in a way that some friends call capricious, some customers even say frustrating. But it all makes perfect sense to me, and I'm always here, so customers can ask me if they don't see what they want, and we can talk about books. And if they really don't want to talk, there's a screen they can use, every volume described, every location listed. But what a shame, to miss a chance to talk about a book.

I'm never in a hurry to go home. The shop is comfortable. There are a few squidgy chairs and a sofa, places where a person can curl up and read. I have a kettle and a coffee machine in the tiny back room. And books are good company.

Well, they're certainly company.

It started a few weeks ago, just after the clocks changed for autumn. Five-thirty and I locked the door, went to make a cup of tea before I updated the data base. When the noise of the kettle stopped I thought I heard movement in the largest side room, nineteenth century novels juxtaposed with later books, similar themes. Had I locked in a customer? No, I checked before I closed the door. Mice? Awful thought: Mansfield Park, Northanger Abbey, Kellynch Hall, chewed to ruins to build a mouse's nest.

I tiptoed my way between the shelves, listened, looked, smelt. No rustles, no droppings, no pungent mouse taint. I decided the noises were those an old building always makes, settling as the evening cools. And promised myself an hour with Val McDermid's take on Northanger Abbey, but not until I'd dealt with the e-work.

The next night all was quiet until after six. I was sitting at the laptop, answering email queries. It wasn't rustling this time. It was murmurs, muttering. Just too quiet to hear the words, but definitely voices.

"Who's there?" I tried to make my voice sharp, not shaky.

The muttering stopped. I switched on all the lights, patrolled the shop, mobile in hand, finger poised to call 999. There was nothing to see, nobody to hear. Couldn't be neighbours, no-one lives in or above the shops next door. Had to be a car radio, I concluded. But all the same, I didn't stop to read that night. I abandoned the emails, scooted out of the shop, hurried home. Next morning I was cautious opening the door, hesitant as I stepped into the shop. Where I found everything as I'd left it. Of course.

That day was month end so I had a couple of accounting routines to run after I'd shut up shop. I left all the lights on, made strong coffee instead of tea, and checked my phone was next to the keyboard when I set to work. I wanted background music, found a Bach concert on the radio. Everything was calm. I worked steadily, entering names and numbers into the spreadsheet, ticking off entries in my handwritten record book.

Until a thump sounded from the side room. The sort of noise a book, falling from its shelf, might make. I froze in my chair. Heard nothing strange, no movement, nobody, just the quiet harpsichord melody from the radio.

But I felt something.

A quick poke into the back of my shoulder. Somebody/something was behind me.

I flinched, gasped, then sank down, hunched, kept my eyes on the screen. Didn't want to turn, didn't want to see, really didn't want to face whatever waited behind my chair.

"What do you want?" My words came out as a whisper, a whisper whose syllables trembled from my lips into the air.

"You have to listen to me."

A woman's voice, a young woman I thought. Slowly I swivelled the chair round, met the eyes of a very young woman. I stared at her.

She wore a grey full-skirted long dress, and round her shoulders she had a black shawl, fastened with a brooch at her throat. Light brown hair pinned into sausage coils around her face. A pretty face, round cheeks, full lips. A mouth that seemed shaped to smile, and trained to smile sweetly; but just now the bottom lip was trembling, the top lip puckered. Hands clasped, entreating.

"They're coming, they'll catch us if you don't stop them. They'll get you too."

"Who are coming?" This ghost, if she was a ghost, was even more frightened than I was.

"I don't know all their names, the worst is called Bill. I heard one of the others call him Bill. But they're all wicked. They're hunting people, people like you and me."

I looked hard at her again, this epitome of a young Victorian miss, before I swivelled to look at my reflection in the timed-out laptop screen. The reflection in the dark glass showed me that my glasses were my most notable feature. Behind them my hair was pulled back into what I knew was a messy bun, and my face showed at least a decade's more wear than my visitor's. I looked down at my long cream jersey, and the charcoal leggings below it.

"Like you and like me how?" Not grammatical, and not in what I'd guess was my visitor's idiom, but she seemed to understand.

"We are both young women, we have some property and

we're defenceless."

Normally I'd argue the defenceless bit, but it wasn't the time, "Who are you?"

"Dora, Dora Spenlow."

The name was familiar. I murmured it to myself, "Dora Spenlow." It came back to me, "Pretty, sweet, little Dora, you marry David Copperfield."

"Do I? He hasn't asked me, but he does seem to like me," her voice tailed off, she smiled.

But her smile vanished at a further thud from the side room. Had another book spilled onto the wooden floorboards in there? The sound was followed, in quick succession, by the clatter of three more tumbles.

I jumped up, backed away from the side room doorway, instinctively held out a hand. Felt Dora, moving beside me, clasp it. Then the sound of footsteps, slow paces across the floor, another crash, more books fell. I couldn't look at Dora, couldn't turn my gaze away from the doorway. My neck was tense, the sinews rigid. Who, what, was coming towards that door?

Then a sudden, loud outburst of applause from the radio. It was followed by the announcer's voice. Calm, measured, appreciative, Ian Skelly brought normality back to the shop. Dora's grasp released my hand. The side room was silent. I could turn my head enough to see that Dora had vanished. I looked back towards the side room, could see nothing past the opening.

But the sharp rap on the shop's outer door made me scream, scream all the screams that had been waiting from the moment the first book fell.

"Lucy, calm down! Lucy, it's me, Jen. Lucy, open the door. Lucy!"

I don't know how long Jen hammered at the door, shouted through the glass, before I heard her voice, and turned towards the front of the shop. I saw Jen's duffle-coated shape, her mittened hands pummelling the glass door, her curls spilling round her horrified face. I fumbled with the lock. Before I could finish opening the door, Jen had pushed in, grabbed me, hugged me.

"What is it? I was walking home, saw the lights were on, so I came over. You weren't moving, just standing, looking back into the shop. So I knocked the window and you screamed, screamed as if," Jen tailed off, then started again. "You wouldn't stop, I was about to ring emergency services. And you're still shaking."

I took a deep breath, tried to halt the long shudders that were stopping me answering, stopping me thinking.

"I need some tea, and you probably want a coffee. But first, will you come with me and look into the side room?"

There wasn't much to see. Just a few volumes on the floor; some Dickens, Hardy, George Eliot. And one by Robert Louis Stevenson, Dr Jekyll and Mr Hyde. That one worried me most.

Jen frowned, looked at me. "What's been going on?"

"A hot drink, then I'll tell you. But you won't believe me."

We sat together, close together, on the sofa. All the lights still on, the radio still playing, while I told Jen about the noises from the side room, and Dora's appearance. She's a good friend, she heard me out, didn't interrupt, never once told me I must be imagining things.

When I finished she took a deep breath, "So I'll come round straight after work the next few nights, stay here with you until you're ready to leave. Give me a chance to catch up on some reading. Lately Matt and I have been watching box sets when we stay in."

There was no arguing with her, and I didn't really want to. We re-shelved the books in the side room, and moved together as we checked each space, switched off lights and walked out of the shop.

"Who is Dora Spenlow anyway?" asked Jen as we walked up the street.

"David Copperfield's first wife. Infantilised character, died conveniently so Copperfield could marry his soulmate," I said tersely.

"Ouch!"

"Sorry, plot spoiler. But she was so sweet, and I keep thinking about what happened to her. And to Dickens's real wife."

"So was Dora killed by this bloke? Bill, you said?"

"No, no I think he's from another book. And it's probably all my imagination."

"Either way, see you tomorrow," Jen gave me a hug as we reached her turning.

The next evening saw us both in the shop. Jen had curled up with a mug of hot chocolate, she was reading the last chapters of Far from the Madding Crowd. I was at the desk, completing the spreadsheet inventory. I had the radio on, Jen had brought a rosemary scented candle – and all the lights were lit. I glanced at Jen, began to feel a bit stupid, and was about to tell her so.

Except that between us, standing placidly waiting for our attention, was Dora.

"Jen, can you see her?"

Dora smiled at me, "Of course she can." She turned to Jen, "Have you come to help?"

Jen gulped, "If I can."

The relief, to know that Jen could also see and hear Dora.

"Dora, can you explain what is happening?" I asked the question gently. Everything about Dora seemed to call for gentleness, for soft voices and kind treatment.

"There are bad people in that room, people who like to hurt, and take. Especially from those who are weaker, and have no protectors, like us."

I think Jen and I had both opened our mouths to argue with her, but a thundering crash from the side room stopped us. A loud shout, then a man's voice demanded, "Where are yer, Flash?"

Dora gasped, ran to hide behind the sofa. Jen and I looked at each other, nodded, and crept towards the open doorway. We saw a heavy-set man pulling at a set of shelves so that he could see behind them. "C'mon. I know you took that sov'rin. Best you give it up easy, then we'll 'ave a look what we can find in this poxy place. Troy and Cass are comin' too."

"Come back Bill, come back do. That Flashman's got a gun, 'e'll 'urt you." A blond woman tugged his arm, but the man didn't turn. He wrenched himself free, then with frightening speed and accuracy lashed back to strike across the woman's face.

"Stop that!"

I didn't know I'd shouted until Bill Sykes looked round at me. Nancy screamed and scuttled back. But Sykes stepped towards me.

"Now 'ere's a bit of entertainment."

It's true, Jen and I both flinched. But then together we stepped forward, grabbed and pushed at the freestanding bookcase. It was heavy, didn't move for one agonising moment, then teetered, wobbled, smashed down onto

151

Sykes. I didn't wait to see more.

I pulled Jen's arm, tugged her back into the main shop, pulling the door shut as we went through it. I heard Sykes' voice behind us, "There y'are Cass. 'Elp me from under 'ere Dunst, then we'll deal with those two. Ain't Troy comin'?"

The closed door didn't stop us hearing the sound of furniture scraping. Jen stepped back, her foot slipped on the book she'd dropped. She looked down and said, "That's weird, I've just been reading about Sergeant Troy's death."

I began to understand what was going on. "Maybe that's why he's not coming to help Sykes?"

The copy of Silas Marner, which had been on the side-room floor the previous evening, lay on my work table. The book had a crack in its binding, I'd put it aside for repair. I rustled through the pages frantically, "It's near the end," I told Jen. And found it. The page where the quarry is drained so they find Dunstan Cass's body, along with Silas Marner's gold.

I tried to ignore the noises from the other side of the door. It sounded as if Cass was struggling to lift the bookcase, Sykes was still trapped. I read the passage aloud to Jen as fast as I could. As I finished we both heard Sykes begin to swear.

"Where you goin' Cass? Come back damn yer."

"That's it," I explained to Jen. "This copy of the book hasn't been read before. So the villain hadn't died. Now I've read it, Dunstan Cass has gone."

"But the other books are still in there." Jen and I looked towards the side room door. It sounded as if Sykes was still trapped, but I wasn't going to open the door to find out.

Jen had a suggestion. "What if we read the books online?"

"I don't think that would work. After all – I've read most of them before. Just not the copies that were on the shelves in that room."

We heard Sykes speak then, "'Oo are you? Come an' 'elp me, for Chris' sake, 'ooever y'are."

And we heard a laugh, a gloating laugh. The sort of laugh a man, or a monster, might make when he saw something helpless, something he could hurt.

"You're on the floor and you can't move. And I'm wearing boots. Marching boots."

Sykes' screams didn't stop us hearing the crunching, squelching thumps. I admit it, Jen and I legged it. I swung the shop door to as we ran out onto the street, but didn't pause to lock it, just ran. We stopped when our legs and breath gave out. We gasped, gulped air, and faced each other under a street light.

I started to speak but Jen shook her head. "I'm coming to sleep at yours. And we'll go back to the shop first thing tomorrow."

We switched on every light in my flat. And kept them on. And the TV. I didn't sleep, but I made myself wait until six before I went into the kitchen. Jen was just behind me.

"It'll be light by seven." I switched on the coffee machine.

"What's that book?" Jen pointed to the volume on the work top.

"I was just checking. It's Stevenson's Dr Jekyll and Mr Hyde. Edward Hyde killed a woman by trampling on her."

Neither of us said anything, just drank our coffee. I kept hearing again the sounds from the previous night, the two men's voices and then the other sounds, trampling, stomping. I thought Jen heard them too.

We walked slowly along the empty road towards the book shop, brightly lit between its dark neighbours. It was too early for anyone else to be about. The shop door was shut.

So many evenings I'd turned back, checked the door was secure before I went home. But it didn't look as if anyone had entered after we'd left. Nothing was disturbed in the front room. The laptop sat on the desk, its charging light silently winking. The candle burned quietly, safe in its glass jar, the smell of rosemary met us as we walked towards it.

Jen and I stayed close together as we stepped to the side room door. We looked at each other, then I turned the handle, pushed. The door opened easily. In front of us we saw tumbled books, the fallen bookcase. But nobody, and, thank heavens, no body.

After we'd picked up the bookcase I persuaded Jen to go home, get cleaned up. She still had plenty of time to get to work. And I knew what I had to do. I'd worked it out through a sleepless night. As I picked up and restacked books I put aside the second-hand ones I'd bought a few weeks previously. They were in perfect condition, had attractive bindings. Someone, I could tell, had bought them to furnish a room. Pristine, unopened, unread.

I've never had any trouble with new books, or with second-hand, well-thumbed ones. But something in that room called to old books; books that languished, stories untold, ideas unexplored, performers given no chance to play their parts. And after a while those characters woke, and stepped out. There was only one way to put them to rest – and that was to read their endings. So I did.

"A couple of things," said Jen, when we met in a café a few weeks later. She has been to the shop again, but only in daylight.

"What things?"

"Well, Flashman, to start with. Why didn't he come back?"

"I'd sold the whole set of Macdonald Frazer's books that day. The buyer thought they'd make a great gift for her

154

father."

"Hope he read them quickly." Jen frowned, "And what about Dora? We abandoned her that night."

"Actually she abandoned us. She came back and told me a few evenings later. Her Doady had found her, hiding behind the sofa."

"Doady?"

"Her pet name for David Copperfield."

"Eugh!" Jen stopped herself, looked at me. "She came back? Didn't you read her story?"

I shook my head. "How could I? She might as well enjoy her life. She didn't want to hurt anyone."

Jen wanted me to come home with her, meet Matt, the person she'd been telling me about for weeks. This time it was serious, she said, they were talking about moving in together. But I made an excuse to leave as soon as I could, then hurried back to the shop.

I hadn't told Jen, but I was expecting visitors.

I've made quite a collection now, of school examination prizes and unopened presents. I store them all on a high shelf in the side room, where customers aren't likely to find them. And I make sure to read all the dénouements, so threatening characters are banished. Which leaves me with all my favourites, the people I've longed to meet and talk with.

That evening I was hoping Albert and Amanda Campion would drop by.

The Race
Paul Hedge

When I was alive I used to wonder what it would be like to be dead. I never realised that I had died many times before. I had forgotten, or rather, I was not allowed to recall what it's like to die and to be reborn. Now that I have passed over yet again, it's all coming back to me. Time has no meaning here. I can't recall how long ago it was since I passed. It feels like only yesterday, which is interesting as yesterday at the moment, no longer exists for me. In the life that I have just left, I was an architect, called Charles Burgess. To my school friends I was known as Charlie Burger. This nickname stuck with me right from my school days, through university and even into adult life.

I can remember the experience you know. Dying that is. I remember every one of my deaths, just as I can remember every one of my lives.

Let me try and explain.

When we are born to a new existence, we cannot recollect anything about our past ones. Yet, after we die, all our memories return to us until we are born again. Even if we have lived many times, we will always remember our past lives at this moment. So far, I have been born six times, which of course means, that I have also died six times. It is through this transitional period of dying and being reborn, let's call it Limbo, that we are allowed to remember our previous lives. It's as if we were deliberately being given the information to make a sort of template for our next life. Our next venture. However, I have to hold my hand up here (if I had one) and say that, what happened before my very first life is a mystery. As it is to all of us. I guess that must have been when I was created.

Of course, the life that I have just left is the most prevalent in my mind at the moment. It was short but so, so sweet! It wasn't a long life. I only made it to forty-two years. You see, I didn't live a particularly healthy life. That was my downfall. My diet was appalling and of course I drank too much. Exercise was none existent, apart from opening the bottle and pouring it into my glass every evening. That said, I had a very happy life. I was married to Enid, I had a fantastic job with my own architectural business, hence I could afford the lifestyle. Good living, beautiful wife, nice home (designed by myself of course) money in the bank and oh, the crème de la crème, my daughter Sophie! She was everything to us; everything a couple could want and I adored her. I probably spoilt her too much but then, hey, that's what fathers do isn't it? Oh how I miss her. Just after Sophie was born, at Enid's request, we bought the land next to us and created a smallholding. Enid was very much into self-sufficiency and enjoyed growing her own food for the family. She had a flock of hens and a couple of pigs. She was in her element but it wasn't really my scene. I hated gardening and I can't stand animals, so, providing I didn't have to help out in anyway, I was content for her to indulge in her hobby. As time went by, Sophie would help out after school and at weekends. She loved it, feeding the chickens and spoiling the pigs. It goes without saying of course that when she became a teenager she wanted a horse. Unfortunately for her, although we had this land, we couldn't accommodate a horse, so she had to make do with riding lessons and borrowing one from time to time from the local stables. We did however have a little extra space and after some undue pressure from the both of them, Enid and I purchased in April this year, an alpaca, which we bought for Sophie's fifteenth birthday. Unfortunately, no one told us that alpacas get lonely and can't live on their own. Apparently, they tend to pine which can even lead to death. So, we had to buy another one to keep her company. Sophie called the male one Punch and female, Judy. We kept them separated by a fence, so that they could nuzzle each other, but that was all. Two alpacas were enough without adding a little one as well. Unfortunately, on a couple of occasions when he was feeling romantic, Punch managed to scale the fence which meant that we had to make it a lot higher. I had an idyllic life. It had, after all, been the life that I had asked and had fought very hard for. I was happy. Enid was the love of my life and so contented with her garden and the animals. Sophie was the child we had always wanted. She was pretty, witty, funny, a joy to be with and doing well at school. Perfect! But I had been so foolish. I allowed myself to become obese, I generally let my health go, I became a Type Two Diabetic and then the inevitable happened and I had a heart attack. A fatal one at that!

So, here I am and just like a game of snakes and ladders, I've again slipped back down the slippery serpent. I'm back at the beginning and about to start a new life all over again! But for the first time I don't want to. I don't want a fresh start. I want to be back with my family. I want to be with Enid and I want to be with my daughter!

We get a choice you know. There are two-hundred-and-fifty-millions of us here and we all get to have a choice. Whether that choice is granted of course isn't always down to us. Luck has a lot to do with it. It took me at least ten attempts to get my first life underway. I didn't ask for anything in particular as far as I remember, because I had never been born before so I had no idea as to what was to come. When the rush came, I just had this instinct to race everybody, beat them to the tape and get the reward of life. That first one wasn't the best life I have to say. I ended up as a daughter to a drunk in New York. In hindsight that's probably where I got my taste for alcohol from. Still, I didn't live very long. I committed suicide, which I didn't realise at the time was a cardinal sin. So, for my second chance, presumably as some sort of punishment, I was held back by the powers that be. I was made a lot weaker and when I entered the race I was last in the rush and too handicapped to win it. I was sluggish, couldn't beat the others and each time I fell by the wayside. Eventually I said I was so sorry for what I had done and could I please be given another chance.

For the next race I was much stronger and I won. The result was, I became the son of a motor mechanic and dinner lady in Walthamstow, London. I was a child in the 1940s and I lived through the blitz, only to get killed by a hand grenade I found lying on the ground on a bomb site in 1952. I was twelve years old. It was an accident, not my fault, so I was given pole position for the next race. This time I asked if I could become a doctor. I didn't think much of my chances but it happened. I was born to aristocratic parents in France and I did become a doctor. I was a good one as well! However, that life was ill timed. It was in the middle of the French Revolution and fell under the influence of a woman... 'Madam Guillotine'.

This was the first existence where I had gone back into time. After this I thought about maybe the Roman era, or even the Middle Ages as I quite fancied being a knight. But I thought of all the illness and pestilence that was around in those days and, having been a doctor, I decided that maybe this choice would not be a wise one. For my next rebirth, I asked to be an ordinary working-class man and I ended up as a window cleaner. It wasn't a bad life. I married and had five sons. Those sons were without exception a pain in backside! Totally lazy and very expensive to keep! We didn't have much money, which was a problem as it meant that I had to work all the hours God sent. Consequently, in my sixty-fourth year, I fell off my ladder and broke my neck. In a strange way, I was quite happy to die and get away from them. For my fifth life, I decided I wouldn't ask for anything. I would just see what came along and take my chance. I ended up a female child star, with very a pushy parent. It was the 1950s, and I first found fame on the radio,

160

aged five. My father would play the piano and I stood by his side looking very cute in a pretty dress, white socks, and ribbons in my hair. Later, my father became my manager and got me a contract with big-band. I hated it. I enjoyed singing, but when the 'swinging sixties' came along, I didn't want to sing the kind of songs he wanted me to sing. He was insistent that I followed his wishes so much so that he had it written into my contract what songs I should sing. So, the inevitable happened and I turned to drugs. I accidentally took an overdose which meant that I only made it to twenty-five. So, this brings me to my last life. For this one I asked only that I'd be successful in business, be very happily married and with a daughter that I would adore. It seemed that even though I have screwed up my last few lives, the power or whatever it is, smiled down on me, because I had a brilliant childhood. It was fantastic from the word go! I married my childhood sweetheart Enid, who I loved very much and together we produced our beautiful baby, Sophie. I adored Sophie from the start, she was the perfect baby, a perfect child and a delightful teenager. My God I loved them both! I didn't want to leave that life; I was so happy. In retrospect, of course I should have looked after my health but I suppose having such a joyous time, I overlooked this very important aspect of my living. Now I face the dilemma of my seventh life. I of course can't go back to my previous one and try again, that wouldn't be allowed. So, after much thought, I have asked to be born within a close proximity to my previous family. So, who would I be? I decided that I would ask to be male, very good looking and with a great sex life. Yes that's right, I want a great sex life! Sex, sex, sex and yet more sex! Why not. I've never asked for that before so it's about time I had a bit more 'rumpy pumpy' in my life! Of course, once I am reborn, I will have no memories of Enid or Sophie. That is all that I want. All I ask is just to be near them. Who knows, maybe, just maybe I might remember something!

I have a good feeling about this request. I know I am only one in two-hundred and fifty million but I am incredibly strong, I have done this before, and I'm confident that I can fight my way through and win the race. I just have to be ready…we never know when it will happen. Hey! I did well! I won the race! It was a tough going though, with some pretty heavy opposition, but I won through. I'm here, nice and cosy, my cells are dividing nicely. Yes, it's all happening again and all I have to do is sit back and wait for about two-hundred and eighty days. Of course, I have no conception of time, all I am aware of is the fact that I am growing bigger by the day. I can't see anything but I can hear muffled sounds.

Something is wrong! I don't know what. Although I don't know night from day, I have a feeling that I had been here for far too long. I don't feel right, not like before and I'm big, very big!

Sophie ran from the garden and into the kitchen. Her mother, Enid, had just finished the washing up.

"Mum! Come and see what has happened! Quickly!" Without waiting for an answer Sophie spun on her heels and ran into the garden. Her mother, dried her hands on the tea towel and followed close on her daughter's heels. Together they made their way to the paddock. Sophie jumped onto the fence and pointed. "Look mum, Judy's had a baby!"

Enid stopped at the fence and looked at the bundle of fur that was struggling to stand.

"Oh, my goodness!" She said, "No wonder! That's why she was putting on weight! I thought Punch had a smile on his face when he broke into her paddock in the spring."

"Isn't he the cutest thing you have ever seen? It is a boy, isn't it?"

Enid laughed, "Oh yes, that's pretty obvious, he's a boy all right!"

"I'm going to treat him special. I'll make sure he has the most beautiful coat; I'll brush him daily and then when he's big enough I'm going to enter him into all the Alpaca shows in the county and win some rosettes! I might even win some money! Isn't he just the best thing ever?"

"Yes darling, he is. What will you call him?"

Sophie thought, but only for a moment. "We'll name him after Daddy, his nickname, we'll call him Charlie Burger!"

Enid smiled. "I'm not sure you father would have liked an Alpaca named after him but in the circumstances, why not?" Sophie grinned at her mother with excitement.

"There's one thing we will have to arrange for Charley Burger first though Sophie."

Sophie look puzzled, "What's that mummy?"

"Male llamas can be a bit sex mad and he's going to be a big boy. Very frisky. So I'm afraid darling we are going to have to get him castrated."

Lost and Found
Nikki Crooks

I pry open my eyes, smack my shrivelled, cracked lips and attempt to peel my tongue from my palate. The Velcro-like sensation causes me to dry-heave. The stale dust from the carpet under my cheek is catching in my throat, which doesn't help. Christ, I feel rough. I have no idea when I crashed out, but I still feel knackered. I squeeze my eyes shut tight in a vain attempt to go back to sleep.

I sit up with a jolt, suddenly compos mentis enough to realise my head should be on a pillow not carpet. Where the hell am I? I frantically look around trying to find my bearings. That's when I see that I appear to be in a hotel lobby. Wearing only a white T-shirt and a pair of tiny black knickers. Oh dear.

Memories of last night are trying to break through the alcohol-induced haze, but to little avail. My attempt to stand up is thwarted by a blinding pain sweeping across my skull, bringing me to my knees. My brain feels like a wrung-out sponge. I bury my head in my hands, waiting for the agony to pass.

So far, I have deduced that I am in a hotel, I am wearing only my delicates and I have a hangover that's making me feel like I've had ten rounds with Tyson. Ok, think. I remember getting to the hotel. I remember the bar. I remember drinking. Anything else? Nope. Do I remember my room number? Nope. I haven't even a vague idea. Bollocks.

Creak. Bollocks, bollocks. Someone's coming. The last thing I need are witnesses to my mortifying predicament. I move as swiftly as I'm able, stumbling as I eventually make it to my feet. The sound of whispered chatter is fast approaching. I get my ass in gear and scurry along the edge of the long corridor, twisting and turning like a lab-rat looking for an escape hatch. I continue round a maze of magnolia paint and Ikea prints for a while, hoping for a glimmer of recognition - something, anything, that will lead me back to my room and my partner in crime, Tara. I assume she made it back to the room and is not currently scuttling about the hotel as I am.

Dread and panic fight for the forefront of my emotions. This is not how I'd pictured a weekend away with my bestie going. I continue to wander staring blankly at doors, sneaking round corners and hiding in doorways to avoid passers-by. Not that there are many. The lack of foot traffic suggests it's still incredibly early.

After a while, dread and panic are replaced with sheer desperation. My only thought is how to get back to the salvation of my room. I need a plan of action. Going to reception is an absolute no-go – chancing having some creepy, nocturnal doorman tweet about a lass rocking up wearing little more than a smile, while passers-by watch as he finds out where I belong is something I really can't deal with right now.

I decide my best chance is to try one of the doors and hope for the best. I imagine rapping on the wood, hearing floor boards creak, the click of the lock turning before Tara peeks out, pulling the door only far enough to see who's disturbing her slumber. I imagine a sigh of relief as my best buddy throws open the door, and her arms, ushering me inside amused but sympathetic. Instead I'm met by a grunt and loud curse from a gravelly voice, followed by the thump of heavy feet on the floor. That is not Tara. I run.

My next guess is more promising. A knock, a shuffle, a mass of blonde hair from behind the door. But again, it is not Tara. I apologise and mumble a lie about sleep-walking, leaving the sleepy stranger bemused. After two more guesses, my drunk-brain becomes aware that this is a terrible strategy. I am back to square one. Bollocks, bollocks, bollocks.

Frustration and anger are now dominant. I plod along until exasperation overwhelms me. I try to fight back tears but it's futile. My legs buckle beneath me and I start sobbing like a kid lost in a supermarket.

After a few minutes I swipe my nose with my hand, and up-turn my t-shirt using the bottom seam to dab my eyes dry. Through misty-eyes I see a beacon of hope. There's a hideous, abstract painting opposite me, and I remember Tara laughing at a particularly phallic looking splodge. Then she turned around and opened…that door there! Number one-two-seven. I'm saved.

Knock, knock, knock.

I hear a clatter inside, "It's four a.m. you twat!" the familiar voice inside shrieks. There's the scuffle of slippers on carpet, then the door flies open. Pure relief engulfs me as I burst past my friend into the refuge of my hotel room. I hear Tara giggle to herself. I am a mess. She looks at me and tilts her head. The tears return. Tara pulls me close to her and consoles me as I describe my humiliating ordeal.

*

Hotel beds are much more comfortable than their floors. I look at the clock: 8.26am. Rolling over, I see a vacant space next to me. A note on the pillow reads, 'You sleep like a corpse. Went for brekkie. Back soon. T x.'

Shame looms over me. My usual tactic of rolling myself in a duvet like a human burrito, watching Dirty Dancing and munching comfort food might remedy this beer-fear. I bundle myself in the soft, white covers, leaving one arm free to operate my tablet and reach snacks. As the movie begins, I can feel a lump rising in my throat and I my chin starts to wobble. Self-loathing is setting in. The water-works begin again.

How do I end up in these situations? I just don't know when to stop, and it always bites me in the ass. Like the time I fell off the bar during a round of fresher's pub golf landing myself in A&E with a broken wrist. That was before realised I was tailor-made for the student lifestyle, however not for a studious life. I bade farewell to university shortly after that incident. Then there was the time I strolled into work three hours late….and still a bit tipsy. That was after Charlie's retirement do. Do you know who knows how to party? People who don't have to worry about work anymore. After that day, I didn't have to worry about work either. Last night epitomises my life: hazy, disjointed, embarrassing.

Baby has just been liberated from her corner, when suddenly a blinding flash dazzles me. I shield my eyes from the light and blink rapidly, trying to rid myself of the white spots impairing my vision. What the hell! There is a hint of a familiar fragrance in the air. My sight is returning to normal, when the scent is accompanied by a voice I vaguely recognise, "Hello Lauren." I look at the source of this intrusion and see a woman standing before me. I stare at her for a while, and she smiles at me, waiting patiently for my response. "Hello?" I finally squeak. She continues to smile at me silently.

"I'm sorry, but who are you? Where did you-? I just saw a flash and-" I say, bewildered, gesturing towards her. She shakes her head and giggles, like a mother laughing at the words of her toddler.

She lets out a long sigh, "Oh, Lauren. I remember this day. What a state. How did that even happen? It's not even the first time we pulled a stupid stunt like this. Remember when we nicked a bottle of Southern Comfort off Tara's mum and

168

necked it in the country park? Then it got dark and we got lost in the woods. That was ridiculous. We thought we'd have eat beasties like in I'm A Celebrity to survive. That was before we were rescued by those two horse riders and it turned out we'd circled round and were only fifteen minutes away from Nan's house." The woman laughed to herself.

How does she know all this? She keeps saying "We". What was she on about? Then it dawns on me. This hangover has really dulled my brainpower. There it is: my dad's nose, my mum's eyes, the little scar on the left cheek. The bits and pieces that make me who I am, are all the bits that make her who she is. Her skin is a little more weathered, there are stray greys in her long, curly hair and her frame is less skeletal than mine, but it is clear as day: she's me.

A plethora of questions flurry through my mind. I can feel her looking at me, watching the cogs turn. She chuckles, "So, the penny's dropped then? Good. Before you ask - how I'm here doesn't matter. I can't tell you. Besides, you'll get it when you're my age, and I don't want to ruin the fun for you." She winks, "As for why I'm here-" She screws up her face and tilts her head as if searching for the right words, then simply states, "Today is not a good day."

Well, no shit Sherlock. Last night was disgraceful. Not only that, it was downright dangerous. Anyone could've found me. I left myself completely vulnerable. I can just imagine pictures of me lying in a heap, wearing only my undies, with make-up smeared down my face all over Facebook - or worse - simply because I like to have a little too much of a good time. This scenario has highlighted exactly what I am: a waster. The type of person that will eventually receive pitied looks by those who have stopped laughing with me and started laughing at me.

Lauren, perches on the edge of the bed next to me. Man, she looks good. Unlike me there are no bags under her eyes, and I can see the contours of her muscles through her shirt.

She looks like she works out. That I cannot fathom. I don't do exercise. I only ever run when I'm being chased.

"Lauren, I'm here to give you a second chance. I'm sorry to tell you today gets worse." Her tone grows serious as she looks at me with concern, "Today is the day you kill yourself."

I'm stunned. I don't know how to respond. She puts her hand on mine and continues, "You'll get home this evening to a letter from your Landlord saying you're getting kicked out, a voicemail from that woman you've been seeing - Kelly, is it? - saying it's over, and a belly-up goldfish. Poor Smarty, may he rest in peace. You'll call dad looking for cash, as we did- as you do. He'll tell you he's cutting you off. He's sick of bailing us out. Says we should stand on our own two feet. That's when you decide you're going to tap out."

I'm trying to take this all in. Homeless, dumped, fishless, skint... Mix that in with the humiliation of today, I can understand my decision. I am so fed up of this rut I've let myself get in to.

Lauren gives my hand a tender squeeze, "I'm here to stop you."

"Why not come when I'm just about to do it?" I ask, curious.

"You're more likely to listen to me right now. Till a moment ago you just had an epic hangover, you didn't know about the other stuff."

I furrow my brow, trying to process all this, "But, if you're here now, doesn't that mean that I don't die? I must survive if you are here with me."

She mimics my expression, "It's complicated. All I can say is everyone deserves a second chance. You'll get the rest later, trust me. And trust me when I say there is a very real chance you could die today."

We both sit quietly for a moment. "So where do we go from here?" I shrug, "If all this shit is coming my way. Why not do it?"

Lauren lets go of my hand and turns up her palms, "At the end of the day, it's your choice. But I'm here to tell you some of the reasons why you should reconsider. You are capable of so much more than you believe."

"Like what?" I ask, trying to hide my cynicism.

"For starters, you stay with Uncle James for a bit. Watching him drink himself into oblivion will be your inspiration for cutting down the sauce yourself." Lauren flashes me a sad smile. I love Uncle James, always the life and soul of a party but I wouldn't be surprised if it got the better of him one day.

Lauren goes on, "A chance meeting at a gig will get you into a job you love. An absolute fluke. You hear two women in the loo having a heart-to-heart about a kid they know. You chip in a bit of advice and spend the evening bantering about what you were like when you were a teenager, and the changes you make. It turns out that one of them is a youth worker, and likes how you 'view the world', as she puts it. She gives you her number, telling you about a vacancy at the centre she works at. You don't know it yet, but you are basically the Teen-Whisperer. They follow you like the Pied Piper."

A feeling of pride stirs inside of me. I haven't even done this yet? How can I feel proud of it? This is stupid. I can barely look after myself, how can I look after other people?

"I know what you're thinking: I can't even look after myself, blah blah blah. But it's true. Then there's the awesome flat you buy with your beautiful wife – wait till you meet her." Lauren says with a grin stretching across her face, "You'll obviously make peace with Dad. He's proud of us by the way. And, you'll realise the world is bigger than Glasgow

171

and visit countries you didn't even realise exist right now. Which is embarrassing to admit. You should already know Iceland isn't just a supermarket."

She takes my hand again, pulls me close and her eyes meet mine, "If you knew how many people think back to when they were twenty-two and want to scream "What were you thinking!", you wouldn't be so hard on yourself. Everybody has a part of their life where they're an idiot. Eventually, they grow out of being an idiot. You are no different. You just take a bit longer to get there. Lauren, we are not special, but we are not losers, we are only human."

She leans forward and kisses me softly on the forehead.

Another flash startles me. I close my eyes against the brightness, and when I open them again, she's gone. My mind is whirring, and my breath grows rapid as hope and fear overwhelm me. I lay back down on the bed, staring at the blank, white ceiling trying to comprehend all I've heard. Exhausted, I fall into a restless sleep.

I'm abruptly awakened by Tara crashing through the door, telling me that it's time to check-out. I quickly cram my things into my rucksack, and head down the lobby. It looks much less intimidating in full day light. And in full clothing.

"How did you sleep?" Tara asks.

"Not bad. I had the weirdest dream though." I say smiling.

Secrets
Andrew Thompson

The aircraft dipped its left wing and started a banking turn. The girl knelt behind the bush, keeping as still as she could. She recognised the bulky shape, the high single wing, the four giant engines; a Hercules. The workhorse of the Royal Air Force, they were always on the news; Afghanistan, Iraq, earthquake relief in Pakistan - they were everywhere. This one had its loading ramp open and as she screwed up her eyes against the sun she saw a lone figure tumble out and begin an erratic descent. She leaned forward to get a better view but lost her balance and fell forwards.

"Who's there?" said the boy, the aircraft in his hand. He held the little paratrooper in his other hand. "How long have you been spying?"

The girl said nothing but dusted the earth off her knees and stood up.

"You have to tell me your name, rank and serial number," said the boy, as the paratrooper hit the ground and the boy tipped it over into a forward roll. "It's in the Geneva Convention."

"I don't have to tell you anything," said the girl, "It's just a stupid game."

"It's a mission," said the boy, "A very important mission." He brought the Hercules down to a bumpy landing on the grass.

"What sort of mission?"

"It's top secret. I can't tell you. You might be a spy."

"Do I look like a spy?"

"Who knows? That's the thing about spies. You can't tell."

"Then anyone could be the enemy," said the girl, "And you

wouldn't know."

"Exactly," said the boy, turning the plastic paratrooper to scan his horizon, "So you trust no-one. Ever." He looked at her. "That's the first thing you have to learn if you're going to really keep anything secret."

Trust no-one. Ever. His words kept repeating themselves in her head as the girl made her way home. She dragged her feet, reluctant to go back into that place. Home, her mother called it. Home! Such a lovely sounding word - warmth, comfort ... trust! She sighed as she thought what other people's homes were like. Well, what they were probably like; she didn't know for sure, because she'd never talked about it with anyone. Maybe she would talk to the boy, if she saw him again.

Everything had been fine until that day. A winter's day like any other, except that Mr Brigham had been ill and after school music had been cancelled, so she'd walked up the tidy front path an hour earlier than usual for a Wednesday. There was a light on in her parents' bedroom, but downstairs was in darkness. Not home yet, she thought, Must have forgotten to switch off the bedroom light this morning. She slipped her key into the Yale lock and opened the door. Something odd. It was warm. And the post was on the hall table, not on the floor. She stopped, and listened. The whirr of the 'fridge, the hum of the boiler - normal everyday sounds, except the boiler shouldn't have been on. The heating was set for five during the week, because everyone was out - she at school, her father at the factory and her mother at the estate agent's office where she was a "sales executive", whatever that meant. She didn't know what it involved but her mother kept telling her father that being a sales executive was a damn sight better than just being a bloody fitter, and heaven knew why she'd ever married him in the first place, let alone stayed with him. It always got worse as the evenings wore on and the red wine went down. Her father never argued; he was a very quiet man, and the girl was sorry for him.

"If it wasn't for her," she'd heard her mother shout through the closed door of the living room late into one night, "I'd have gone long ago. Long ago. I could have...." But she hadn't heard any more because her father had opened the door and seen her sitting on the bottom stair. He took the girl in his arms.

"Pay no heed," he'd said, "She doesn't mean it. She's .... tired. Working too hard at the agency. Ought to go to bed, but you know your mum. Knows her own mind."

Then there'd been a crash from the lounge followed by her mother's voice:

"Michael? Michael? You there? Be a love and bring us another bottle. The Shiraz."

Her father had rolled his eyes. "Off you go, Princess. Up the apples and pears. She'll be fine tomorrow; you know how she is. She loves you, you know."

The girl had nodded, tears on her cheeks. Of course she did. Didn't all mothers love their daughters?

And then it was that day and she was at the foot of the stairs again, listening to a sound she couldn't quite identify, a sort of animal sound. Almost a low growl but mixed with squeals of...what? It sounded like pain, or terror, she couldn't be sure. She could hear movement, and now someone was shouting No! No! and the screams were getting louder, and more frequent.

"Mummy?" she called, in a voice that quivered with fear,

"Mummy? Is that you?"

The noises stopped and the house was silent for a moment, then she heard a rustling sound and the bedroom door opened to reveal her mother in a dressing gown.

"Holly," said her mother, "I wasn't expecting...I thought you were at...it's only four fifteen."

"Music was cancelled. Mr Brigham's ill." The girl, Holly, paused. "Mum, is everything OK? I thought I heard...I thought maybe there was someone...I thought I heard voices."

"Voices?" said her mother, "Of course not. Don't be silly."

"But I heard something. And a man's voice. I'm sure."

"Nonsense," said her mother, "I had the telly on. That's all." Her mother thought for a moment. "I had to come home from work early. Bad headache. I...Holly...be an angel and run down to the shop for me. We need some bread. There's money in my purse."

Holly stared at her mother. Her purse? She'd never been allowed in her purse before. She hesitated.

"And Holly, there's no need to say anything to your dad about my being unwell. You know how he frets. Our little secret, just between you and me. OK?"

As Holly had closed the gate behind her two things had struck her: her mother's lipstick had been smudged, and the blue Subaru parked in the road outside their house was just like the one her mother's boss drove.

She saw the boy again, playing with his 'plane, only this time it was being pursued by a small fighter; the Hercules was in his left hand and the jet in his right. The noises he was making were not very realistic, she thought, but they seemed to work for him.

"Hullo," she said, when it looked like the Hercules couldn't possibly escape from the pursuing jet.

"Hello."

"How's your secret mission?"

"If I told you, I'd have to shoot you," he said.

"I've got a secret, too," she said, "And I've never told anyone."

"A real secret?" he asked.

"A real secret. Not a pretend one like yours."

"What is it?"

"It's a secret. How can I tell you? I promised someone. If I tell you, it won't be a secret anymore, will it?"

But she wanted to tell him. She had carried the burden of that day for three months, and she hated it. She saw her father following her mother around like a puppy, always anxious to please, and how did she treat him in return? Like dirt. It wasn't fair. And Holly was part of it. She had kept the secret. Her father had no idea.

She had seen the Subaru outside the house again, and each time she had gone to the park and waited until she thought he'd be gone. And each time had felt more guilty that she was allowing it to happen.

And now she was back in the park and there was someone here who knew she had a secret and she couldn't tell him what it was.

"Go on," said the boy, "Promise I won't tell. Honest."

She could sense the excitement in his voice at the prospect of sharing a genuine secret, and she knew she would feel better if she shared it. She swallowed.

"OK then," she said.

They sat on the ground while she told her story. She fidgeted as she talked, her fingers plucking at blades of grass or feeling the smooth contours of the edging stones that separated the lawns from the flower beds. The boy didn't interrupt her. She spoke flatly, without emotion, as she told him about that day and that man. The only time her voice betrayed her feelings was when she spoke about her father, and how she had kept the secret only to protect him.

"But now I've told you," she said, "So it's not a secret anymore, is it?"

"'Course it is," said the boy, "I'm not going to tell anyone, am I?"

The girl looked around her. Satisfied, she gripped one of the edging stones she had been stroking earlier.

"No, you're not," she said, bringing the stone down sharply on the boy's head.

For a moment his eyes showed pain and surprise.

"Trust no-one," she whispered, as the life ebbed from the boy's body, "Ever."

Mr Basset and the Abseiling Alien
Angela Wilson & Matt Smith

Mr Matthew Basset's paws felt leadlike on the doormat, as he hauled himself out behind her. Two weeks ago, his little human had had a birthday party, and was now a "teenager".

Last week, what a nightmare! She'd barely spoken to him, glued to her phone. When they reached the seafront cliff path, she'd plonked herself down on one of the rock benches, let him off, and shooed him away. He'd tried licking her hand, but she was back to that stupid phone again. Grr!

Today seemed destined to be the same sorry affair. Except as he trudged down the cliff walk, he refused to look back. For a while he could smell that new perfume of hers, an assault on the nostrils, if ever there was one.

He was trying to keep a stiff upper muzzle, yet he couldn't help but hang his head. He couldn't even be bothered to sniff at things today.

If he were a dog given to hyperbole, he might say the rough path was a magnet threatening to pull his heart to it. Instead, he tasted the bittersweet nip of nostalgia along with the salty sea air, picturing Shelly arriving home from the hospital, tiny and bundled up in a cosy blanket. Though he was a good boy and did not jump up on her, he'd sworn to himself there and then he would be her number one protector.

Watching her grow had been the most joyous thing. He hadn't even minded when she was going through her toddler rebellion phase and would constantly tug at his ears. And the adventures they'd had together! Well, had he had fingers, he swore he could've written a book. They were the best of friends and he'd always felt like the luckiest Basset in the world. He loved it when she would proudly show off "My Basset" to all and sundry, wrap her little arms around him, and hug him. She would always sneak him bits of her food too. They truly were the dynamic duo.

Then, for the last year or so the most exciting thing yet. Shelly had been allowed to take him for walks on her own, so Sunday afternoon had been their sacred time. After lunch they would fly out the door together and the fun times would roll.

Permitting himself a smile, he cast his mind back along the evolution of his name. He'd been "Muh Buh", when Shelly was learning to speak. Then "Bat Hound" when she became yet more articulate. Then he was "Matt Bass" for a bit (as it sounded cool, apparently). Then finally, in a dog show when she was ten, she entered him as, "Mr Matthew Basset Hound Esquire". This had made them both feel very grown up. They'd even won second prize, the judge praising his strong feet and shiny lemon white coat. Shelly had kept the blue rosette on his collar for weeks.

And now…what had his best friend evolved into? She probably wouldn't notice if he actually turned into a lemon and white rosette! Did she even care for him anymore? This feeling like a burden totally sucked. No, he wouldn't look back. He needed what was it the humans called it? A distraction. Hmm. Normally Shelly and he would be so busy having a laugh, and larking around, he wouldn't bother looking up and about much. He craned his neck though, and was surprised to see lots of people in orange jumpsuits scaling down the red chalky cliff. Mr Basset watched as they skirted patches of tiny yellow flowers and blue solar squares. They were spritzing the parched, crumbly earth with a big plunger that went 'squoosh'. It was like a larger version of those scented bathroom sprays. He sniffed the air, was that his favourite juicy bone? He flapped his ears about, carrying the scent more intensely to his nose. Now, that was what they should make perfumes out of.

He pushed on, upping the pace as a bracing wind ruffled his

fur. He gave a cursory nod to an oncoming spaniel. Passing through a gate that said, "DOGS MUST BE ON A LEASH", he considered peeing on it; instead going with a two claw salute. Then he found himself peering down the flight of steps that led to the railway tunnel. Suddenly all the orange jumpsuits came streaming up. He glanced over his shoulder at the empty cliff face. Wow! How did they…? And where were their ropes and harnesses? Come to think of it, what ropes and harnesses? They were all about seven feet tall and he felt lost in a sea of bright amber. He clenched his muscles, jaws to paws. Then an orange jumpsuit crouched down and scratched Mr Basset's head.

'Hello old chap. What are you doing by yourself? Are you lost?'

Mr Basset couldn't help but wag his tail.

'Thank you for thinking of me Mr Orange Jumpsuit Man. I do know where I am, geographically, yet I'm feeling lost in myself. I just don't know what my role is anymore.'

'I know exactly what you mean. Life is a weird one, eh?'

As Mr Orange Jumpsuit removed his hard hat and ruffled his hair, Mr Basset peered at him. Then he shook his chops, his tail going again.

'Wow. I thought I'd seen, heard, and sniffed it all. But, for the love of Dog, I never knew humans could speak Canine or have orange horns.'

'They don't,' chuckled Mr Orange Jumpsuit, 'but, you see I'm actually a visitor to this planet. We're here on a working holiday, if you like.'

'Are you an alien?' Mr Basset's eyes were flying saucers. He knew of aliens; he and Shelly had a watched programme where this floppy haired fancy pants science guy had banged on about them.

181

'Eh-lee-ann?' Mr Orange Jumpsuit scratched his horns, and laughed again, 'well, yes, I suppose I am. But you can call me Criss Cross.'

Hmm, that name did seem to suit him. He'd first clapped eyes on him criss-crossing down the cliff face, after all.

'Pleased to meet you. I'm Mr Matthew Basset Esquire.'

'Very pleased to meet you.'

As Criss Cross shook his paw, Mr Basset clocked orange fingernails.

'But, hey little guy, you seem very troubled. Can we help you at all?'

Mr Basset glanced over his shoulder. He regretted his earlier outpouring of emotion, not very Basset. And I mean, who were these big dudes? Could he trust them? He wished there were some grass to chew on.

Criss Cross unscrewed one of his horns, put it to his mouth, and spoke through it:

'Take a break guys and gals; I'll meet you down at HQ in five!'

Dutifully all the orange jumpsuits turned and filed back down the steps. As he watched them go, Mr Basset pondered whether they all had orange communication horns hiding under their hats, or just Criss Cross?

'That's better', said Criss Cross, eyes sparkling, 'I forget we can be a bit full on, en masse.'

Criss Cross settled onto a handy rock bench, and placed his hat down. Mr Basset came and sat nearby.

'Beautiful planet you have here.'

'Yeah, I suppose it is.'

Mr Basset looked out across the bay. His eyes found the

cave where he and Shelly had once sheltered, laughter and howling mingling in a cacophony of echoey delight.

'Can I ask you something?'

'Of course.'

'What were you all doing on the side of the mountain? And what was that spray thing? I swear it smelt like my favourite bone.'

'It did?' Criss Cross jumped up, and clapped his hands together. Mr Basset nearly cracked up. It reminded him of a tiny excited Shelly.

'Mr Basset, that is brilliant news! It means it's working…the spray is working. You smelt your favourite thing! Oh, the others are going to be made up.'

As Criss Cross gazed at the steps, Mr Basset noted a smile as warm as his amber horns.

'What sort of spray is it though?'

'Oh right, context!' laughed Criss Cross, 'Sorry, It's an empathy spray.'

'Come again?' Mr Basset cocked his head.

'You see we are from the planet Empath.'

'M-Path? Like Cliff Path?'

'Empath with an E, like empathy. Us Empathians possess an innate ability to understand one another's feelings. That's why I had to think for a minute, when you asked me to explain it. We don't generally have to do that for each other, because we already get it.'

'Oh. That sounds like a great skill.'

Criss Cross kneaded long fingers.

'It is, as a rule. However, we have reached a point in our evolution where things almost come a bit too easy for us.

We've hit an empathic ceiling, if you like.'

He pressed amber thumb nails to his lips.

'Hence we want to progress; need new challenges. A great way to start, we decided, would be to travel to different planets, offering help to other societies and civilizations who perhaps don't relate to each other quite as well.'

Now it was Mr Basset's turn to burst out laughing. He looked up to see Criss Cross studying him carefully.

'Sorry! Only your timing couldn't be better. It's a total nightmare between my human Shelly, and me. We used to be a bit like you guys. We were the best of friends, understood each other through and through…'

'And now?'

'Now, it's like she's alien to me. No offence.'

'None taken. Has she just become a teenager, by any chance?'

'How did you guess?'

'Well, Mr Basset, teenage brains are an enigma in any species.'

'Do you have a teenager?'

'I did,' Criss Cross narrowed his eyes, 'and though we may be a race of Empaths, even our teenagers are dreadful communicators, moody, silent and mysterious. Half the time, they don't even know why. Their hormones are going haywire. They're trying to grow into themselves, see?'

Mr Basset wrinkled his snout. Shelly had once shown him his puppy pictures. He was all balloon ears and big paws, not quite grown into himself. Was Shelly going through the equivalent of this now?

'Change feels strange.'

Criss Cross nodded vigorously.

'Try not to take it too personally, with your little human, though. I know it may seem like she's freezing you out, but I'll wager she'll need you now more than ever.'

'Do you reckon?'

'I do, Mr Basset. I do. But she'll need you in a different way to how she has done before. It may require some change of approach on your part also. Space and support will be key.'

Mr Basset gazed up at Criss Cross's glowing horns.

'Forgive my ignorance Criss Cross. I understand support, but, when you talk of space, do you mean your sort of Space? Planets and stuff?'

Criss Cross reached down and scratched Mr Basset's head.

'It means you have to let her be by herself, in a proxemic sense. I know it seems counter intuitive, when all you want to do is protect her, but that growing into herself she needs to do? She needs a bit of her own space to do that, sometimes.'

Mr Basset frowned at the ocean. By herself? Separate from him? He wasn't sure if he could do that. They'd always been together, always.

Although, come to think of it, last night she'd slammed her bedroom door in his face.

"Get out Mr Basset, this is private!"

He'd slept wedged against her door anyway, like one of those long draught excluder things. The only time he'd been on his own, was after a trip to the Vet. He had just wanted to lay in a dark room by himself. Shelly had lasted precisely three minutes before coming to "check" on him. Even then, he'd not pushed her away. Was it like this now for her? But, she wasn't poorly was she?

'Remember, it won't always be that bad though,' Criss Cross cut through his train of thought, 'the teenage years won't last forever. Eventually she'll come out the other side. Change is scary, I know. But, for what it's worth, I don't think the strong bond you two share will be broken. Tested and changed, maybe, but never severed.'

'That's the thing though,' Mr Basset felt cold, steel jaws clamping his heart, 'I'm fourteen now. That's twilight years for a Basset. What if I don't come out the other side? Who's going to watch over Shelly and take care of her, then?'

Criss Cross patted the seat beside him, and Mr Basset heaved himself up. He stretched out, chin on paws.

'I feel bad, too. I realise now I've been selfish. I've been constantly pestering Shelly for attention, wanting things to stay the same; no thought to what she may be going through. How scary all this might be for her.'

Criss Cross stroked Mr Basset's head. Mr Basset swore his horns shined even brighter orange.

Mr Basset shook himself. Had he been asleep? He peered up to see Criss Cross beaming down at him, dazzlingly orange in the dim light.

'Ok old chap?'

Where…? Some sort of cave, he reckoned. Red and yellow shimmer merged with Criss Cross's amber sheen. The ice around Mr Basset's heart had melted. He felt hopeful.

'Now, I hope you don't mind me teleporting you. We're under the railway bridge in a little cavern. We've been using it as temporary HQ whilst we're here.'

'Oh, ok. Cool.'

Mr Basset stretched out his stubby legs, unrushed, as Criss Cross went on.

186

'I've had a chat with the others, and we want to offer you a reward, see? I was so impressed with your empathy today. The way you looked at your own behaviour with absolute selfless compassion for your young human. We totally decided you should be the one.'

Mr Basset wrinkled his snout.

'Umm, might need a little more…'

'Context? No probs.'

Criss Cross crouched down, meeting his eyes with a smile.

'Remember we were chatting about our cliffside work, and our empathy spray?'

Mr Basset hopped up, all ears.

'Yep, you said the fact I smelt my favourite bone showed it had worked.'

'Indeed. You see, we were actually mining the side of the chalky cliff.'

Criss Cross scratched his horns. A sheepish look played about his amber eyes.

'I hope you don't think that is selfish, or stealing? We were careful only to take a little bit. We only wanted to see if you guys had any natural resources here that we don't back home which we could use to improve the formula.'

Mr Basset nodded - seemed a fair exchange. Could Criss Cross already tell he thought that, though, and was just checking as a courtesy? This idea crinkled the corners of his muzzle up into a smile.

'And then, after we mixed some of the minerals in, the spray empathising with you by sending you your favourite scent, meant we were definitely onto something.'

'That is so cool. And good undercover work I reckon. Nobody questions what you're doing in an orange jumpsuit.'

'Glad you approve Sir,' Criss Cross gave a conspiratorial wink, 'we are absolutely delighted. However, as I say, we didn't want to help ourselves to your supplies, without giving something back.'

Mr Basset cocked his head. His new friend's feet may be pacing up and down but where was he going with his words?

'As we, as a species, prize empathy above all else, we fully intended, when the formula was perfected, to reward someone who demonstrated exemplary understanding of the feelings of another.'

Mr Basset could hear his heart pounding in his floppy ears.

'So what do you say, Mr Matthew Basset Esquire? Fancy a spritz with our new improved Empathy Longevity Mist?'

As he pelted out of the shady tunnel, paws pounding up the steps, he gulped at the hazy air; it tasted decidedly youthful. The foamy waves crashing against the broken rocks below kept pace with his thumping heart. Criss Cross had explained that the improved empathy mist spray now contained a longevity element, meaning Empaths could continue their great work for longer. Mr Basset had briefly worried that he wasn't worthy. What if the 'exemplary understanding' he'd shown was just the spray talking, as he'd caught scent of it on the cliff path? Criss Cross had assured him, however, that his empathy indisputably derived from within.

He couldn't quite believe his luck; he was so happy to be a guinea pig - guinea dog? Whatever! As long as he could support Shelly through her weird and wonderful teenage years, anything else was a bonus. A big, juicy 'bone-us'!

He saw Shelly waiting for him down the path. Though it took all his self-control, he didn't rush at her.

'Let her come to me,' his head told him, 'space, support, and empathy.'

Standing back, as he was though, he could see the worry etched across her lovely features. And there it was, a glimpse of the little girl he once knew.

Then she rushed straight at him, flinging her arms around him.

'Mr B, you massive numpty! Where've you been? You nearly gave me a heart attack.'

As he snuggled into her, contentment seeped through every fibre of his fur.

Shelly then pulled back, eyeing him curiously.

'Am I getting older, or do you look younger, boy?'

She laughed as he barked happily, then her blessed phone pinged.

'Oh look Mr B, Sammy's texted me. He is so cool!'

Mr Basset wasn't sure whether to roll his eyes, or crease up laughing, as he followed Shelly back down the path. Ah heck, so what if the energy of growing was currently sapping her empathy, he had plenty enough for both of them. And though he now understood he couldn't wrap his blossoming little human in a protective mist forever, how 'out of this world' that he would still be here by her side for these formative years, all thanks to an abseiling alien and his magical spray.

A Sting in the Tale
Taria Karillion

"DON'T touch that!"

"But, Muuuum, it's - "

"Don't 'But, Mum' me! That is not a ball, so don't even think about kicking it! Now, leave it exactly where you found it and come here before you get hurt! You know you shouldn't touch or disturb anything before we've set up the safety equipment!"

The boy pouted and huffed, then stomped away from where the odd-looking almost-sphere was hanging. His mother hauled him aside and stabbed the air with her finger as she spoke.

"Now, listen - that thing is a home to millions of tiny creatures. They may be miniscule, but if even a few of them got you, you'd know about it, and that could be you in a whole lot of pain and hours in some godforsaken excuse for a hospital! We've told you before – when you're in a foreign place, you have to be extra careful with the wildlife. They might be poisonous, even!"

The boy tried hard not to roll his eyes. Being home-schooled was cool except for times like this when he had to hang around dull study sites in the middle of nowhere for hours while his parents and other nerdy scientists crouched around specimens in their weird camouflage gear, whispering into recording equipment and taking icky samples.

"Anyway," his mother continued, "even if they weren't dangerous, I've not brought you up to be cruel! How would you like it if some giant came along and lifted up our home, or poked at us with a stick? Have you learned nothing about respecting the habitats of endangered species?"

191

"Endangered?" The boy squinted up at his mother. "I don't understand – we've seen loads of these!"

"Well, yes, I know, but this colony is an exception. Their species usually evolve to function as a focussed hierarchy of rulers and workers. They gather, store and distribute food in a highly ordered and fair way, and because of that they've survived for a very long time. But - " she shook her head, "…But, for some reason, this particular variety are bafflingly uncooperative and self-destructive. That's why we're all here – to study why they've become that way."

"Stupid things." the boy mumbled, glowering at the intricately patterned, almost spherical lump of brown and grey. "Why do we have to come on these stupid field trips, anyway? Why can't we have a proper holiday like other families?" He emphasised his displeasure by thumping the nearest all-terrain vehicle repeatedly with each muttered syllable.

"It's just - not - fair!"

"I heard that!" the mother frowned. "You know very well why we're here – you can either come with your parents on these expeditions and we can be together as a family, or you can go live in a boarding school or with a relative. But we far prefer the former." She gave a sad sigh, her voice and expression softening.

"Look, your education isn't just about academics, son – it's about what we learn from each other - how best to behave - or not behave - in society, to benefit from our strengths and protect ourselves - and others - from our weaknesses." She glanced at the little habitat. "And – hopefully – how to show enough compassion to others to understand them, and help them out, before it's too late. That's a far better use of our time than just lazing around in a pool somewhere, don't you think?"

She patted him on the shoulder with a smile, He shrugged

and nodded, then watched as she continued to take measurements, pictures, recordings, observing the object from all angles.

"But Mum… I'm bo-o-o-ored." he mumbled.

"Have you finished your current homework?" came the answer.

"Um… no. We've got to write a stupid history essay on 'Superseded Cultures'. But … well, I don't even know what that means! Do I have to do it? "

His mother looked up from her microscope and gave him a stern look.

"Son, the only reason you've been allowed to come on this field trip is that you have that expensive, digital tutoring service. If that's not working out, we can always send you back home to stay with your Aunt, so you can attend a regular school. Do we need to do that?"

"Mum! No! … Oh, alri-i-i-ight, I'll get on with it – but, can you at least just give me a clue?"

"Well, you've got a very good example with these little guys right here!" She stretched out an arm but was met with a blank look. Taking a deep breath, she pointed and carried patiently on.

"This particular sub-species has problems that may well lead to it being superseded. There's an imbalance in the population – they have a large number of advanced, specialist workers – like drones? They have the sole purpose of tackling whatever threatens the colony – normally predators, but in this case it's a polluted water supply and food scarcity – because of overpopulation. Unfortunately, there may soon be more of the drones than the original population, and because the drones are more industrious and intelligent than their predecessors, they could eventually dominate the whole colony and impose their own rule, superseding the older subjects, even replacing them, in order to achieve the goal that they were made to achieve."

"Woah…" the boy's eyes widened. "Harsh!"

His mother held up her arms.

"It's just basic logic, son, and sometimes that is harsh. Now, it looks like the team have finished setting up the Hide, so bring me the magnifying lens, and come with me. Move slowly and gently so you don't disturb them, and make sure the protective netting and camouflage is properly in place. The weaker ones might die of sheer fright if they see the size of us!"

He followed her with a look of genuine curiosity as she beckoned him inside.

"Hush now… Look, there? Can you see from the different colours of the outer surface where the drones have repaired and rebuilt the damaged and decayed parts? And that's great for species longevity and colony survival. But - and this is a big but (no, stop sniggering, don't be rude!) – these drones are intelligent enough to know that those repaired areas will only stay intact if the non-drones are kept away. So, they herd them into other, smaller parts of the habitat. Like ghettos in cities? But those groups are so self-destructive that they'll eventually die out."

"I don't get it, Mum … isn't that just survival of the fittest? 'And isn't that a good thing?"

"Shhh – whisper!" she chided, then gave a philosophical shrug.

"That depends on whose perspective you look at it from, son. From our point of view, probably, yes. But there are millions – maybe even billions - of a tiny species down there who would probably disagree, if they had the intelligence to be aware of what they're doing to themselves."

She ruffled his head and smiled. "Now, enough chatter! Please pass me that sample holder and extraction tool and then you can go and finish your essay. After that you can explore for a while – but stay close – in sight of the camp - and no touching anything you can't name! I'll join you for food when I've filed my report. Speaking of which, where did I put my recorder?"

The boy slunk off as she found her equipment and headed to the command centre, recorder in hand.

"Project T-52567: Progress report…I regret to confirm that it is indeed as we thought – this little colony is very nearly beyond our help. Even my brief, initial assessment showed significant contaminant damage and widespread evidence of colony breakdown. It's therefore likely that internal battles of dominance will be likely to pose more of a threat than that from natural predators.

Also, the newer drones appear vastly more evolved than the original inhabitants – more so than we anticipated. It seems they have made significant improvements and repairs to the habitat shell and territory immediately beyond. However, it is our belief that the drones may eventually determine that their predecessors are in fact the source of the problem, and may, therefore, supersede and enslave, or even – quite logically - eradicate them."

Pausing for a moment, she glanced across the site between her milling colleagues, to where the ATVs were parked. Checking that her son was safely inside, hunched over his computer, she added,

"Also, query whether the Schools Liaison Department might find it valuable to cite this study as an example of sociological breakdown in a microcosm, and how we could learn from them. Further notes on this to follow in a subsequent report."

A short while later, a hot drink and a snack slid under the protective netting.

"Aw, thanks son – that's kind. I really appreciate your support. Did you finish your essay?"

"Yes, Mum. I'll send it as soon as I've double checked it."

Without looking up from her magnifying lens, his mother answered,

"Ok – well done, kiddo. Make sure of your spellings, eh? And remember to add that this sub-species is endangered."

"Ok, Mum… It's 'h-u-m-A-n-s', right?"

Saving the Whales
Jane Bheemah

Huddled in her anorak, Emma shivered. Joining a local group for a spot of beach cleaning was one of those things that had seemed like a fun idea at the time. However, on a chill October Sunday the reality was proving rather different. It had been a shock to learn Pete wasn't coming. After all, it was his passionate talk that had made her sign up for it in the first place. Well, Emma acknowledged, that and a pair of penetrating, hazel eyes set in the most drop-dead gorgeous male face ever. Tall and lean, his chiselled features suggested film star, rather than the post-grad student he said he was. Her artist fingers had itched to draw him- - - after they'd done other things together first, of course.

Recalling the evening she'd opened her parents' front door and found the earnest young man on the step campaigning for 'Friends of the Earth,' Emma felt a different sort of shiver down her spine. They'd chatted for ages. If her father hadn't been at home, she would have invited him in for a coffee. Unfortunately, her Dad didn't hold with what he called 'new-fangled ideas.' In his opinion, climate change was a myth. The world would keep on turning just as it had done for eons, with or without human meddling. A verbal clash would have been both inevitable and embarrassing.

She'd been looking forward to today, counting the hours. Except that now Pete wasn't here. 'Meet me by the gift shop, we'll walk down together,' he'd said. She'd hung around for ages before venturing down on the pale, sandy beach, hoping to find him. No sign. What a let- down! She hated broken promises. Seeing a straggly group forming, she'd joined them and asked around. And discovered Pete wasn't coming. Apparently, he'd had been called away on an important mission. A whale watch with Green Peace, she thought she heard someone say. A last-minute opportunity to go. He was attached to so many different, environmentally friendly groups, Emma thought the explanation sounded quite likely.

The grey sky mirrored her mood. She wondered if Pete realised, wherever he was, how much she missed him. The earlier fizz of excitement had dissipated, leaving her flat. However, she was part of the group now – roped in and corralled. Giving the organiser her name, Emma donned gloves and accepted the large rubbish sack thrust at her. The task ahead felt daunting. She had to keep reminding herself what a useful service this was.

Left with only the geeky types to talk to, Emma stomped across the sand. Minus Pete, she didn't feel inclined to be sociable. All the joy was sucked from the day. Taking a glance at the rest of the group, she decided to gradually distance herself. It was going to be a long afternoon, but she'd rather scour the beach for litter on her own. Maybe she wasn't cut out to save the planet, or anything else for that matter. Her thoughts drifted. Maybe she ought to swop her 'A' Level choices, like Pete suggested. Switch from English, Art and Design, soft subjects, to more practical options, like geography and environmental science – if the college would allow. The autumn term had begun, but students did change options.

True, those subjects weren't her strong suit. But with a bit of effort, perhaps - Trouble was, she was in her second year. Also, she loved art and didn't want to drop it. Pete was quite right, though. She could always draw and paint as a hobby. He'd been encouraging her to try politics, too. Take up a Green Party membership. The world needed forward thinking, environmentally savvy politicians like her, he'd said. She had a duty.

Emma had been uncertain, but he'd said the Party was crying out for new blood. Oh, they might be a mere pressure group now, but all that was poised to change – once people woke up and realised the planet was dying and they were sleep walking into oblivion. Did she read the Bible? Hadn't she heard of Armageddon? Well, that day was not far off. Truth be told, images of mass destruction had given her nightmares. Pete could be scarily intense.

Picking up yet another discarded sandwich wrap, Emma sighed. When would the public learn to take their picnic debris back home? How much education did it take, for goodness sake? All it needed was for everyone to be responsible for their own stuff. Then events like this wouldn't be necessary – and she'd be curled up at home, snug in her room with a book. Glumly, Emma surveyed the wide expanse of bay that was Praa Sands. It was an ebb tide. Beautiful in season, the flat Cornish beach now looked bleak and forbidding. Briefly, she wondered if she could sneak away unnoticed. But what would they tell Pete then?

Delving in her jacket pocket for a sandwich, she carefully unwrapped the grease proof paper – then yelped as a large gull swooped, black beady eyes focussed on her food. Before she could act, the tasty snack had been deftly removed from her fingers. Up close, wings flapping and squawking noisily, the bird's yellow beak looked vicious. Emma shuddered. Not for the first time she wondered why gulls, who seemed a match for anyone, were a protected species. She determined to ask Pete. To her mind, they were a scourge.

The salty wind stung her cheeks, at the same time lifting a nearby empty Cola bottle. Catching it, Emma felt a brief sense of victory. One more piece of plastic she'd saved from going in the ocean! Sea creatures swallowed these indigestible bits of plastic, that was the problem. Then cast-off wrappings or whatever else they'd swallowed twisted round their gut. Emma frowned in distaste, recalling Pete telling her how easy it was for fish to choke to death - leave aside the damage plastic could do to the environment in other ways.

He'd shown her graphic images of the inside of a shark's stomach - made her feel quite sick, truth be told. Apparently, the animal had died from intestinal obstruction, mirroring the fate of other marine creatures. Trying to lighten the mood, she'd suggested that killing the odd shark might not be such a bad thing; safer waters to swim in and all that.

Pete hadn't laughed. Instead, he had looked horrified. Sharks, he'd explained, had a most important role; they were like the dustbins of the ocean. Top predators in their natural environment. Powerful and streamlined, they cleaned up the seas and kept everything in balance. At least, they had done until humans came on the scene, messing things up with their selfishness and complete disregard for other species.

Plastic didn't biodegrade, that was the real issue, he'd told her. It built up over hundreds, if not thousands of years, clogging the Earth's eco-system. The scientists were working on it, Pete said, but they were light years away from coming up with a solution. People needed to change their behaviour and stop using so much of the stuff. It wasn't necessary. Three quarters of supermarket wrapping could be done away with, probably more. If you dwelt on things too much, Emma had said, you'd end up quite depressed. After all, what could one person do? Plenty, Pete has responded – like join in a beach clean!

Feeling duly chastened, she'd signed up to be here today. No excuses - everyone needed to do their bit for survival of Mother Earth. Pete was spot on; it would be tragic if our beautiful Blue Planet died for want of initiative. Kicking an empty sardine can with a nasty, jagged edge, she wondered where he'd gone for this whale watch. Somewhere more exciting than Praa Sands, no doubt! Funny how it had been so last minute, though. She'd have expected that sort of trip to be organised months in advance.

It could be a ruse, of course. Maybe he'd had a peek at the

weather and decided to stay indoors and leave the minions to do the work. Cosy up with a girlfriend, if he had one – which obviously she hoped he didn't. Emma sighed. He was out of her league. A good-looking guy like Pete was bound to have a girlfriend tucked away somewhere. Another clever uni student, probably, who had followed him on this whale watch.

Drop dead gorgeous blokes like Pete weren't available to ordinary girls like her. She'd been daft to get her hopes up. Unless he was gay, of course - but then he'd have a boyfriend. Anyway, she was here now, regardless. So, best make the best of it and get this community beach clean thing over with. Head down, Emma scanned the ground beneath her feet, the organiser's promise of hot coffee at the end spurring her on. That, and the thought someone in authority might tell Pete what a help she'd been.

Brightening, she imagined Pete seeking her out and saying something like, 'Great start for a newbie, I hear, Em. Sorry I couldn't be with you.' Then he'd take her for a coffee to make up for his absence and tell her all about the whales – which hopefully he'd managed to save. She rather liked whales. In fact, she'd drawn one during her last art class. Magnificent creatures, well worth saving!

Emma closed her eyes, imagining Pete finding them a cosy little bistro. It wouldn't be long before he leaned over and brushed her lips with a kiss, saying he couldn't help himself. She attracted him too much to resist. Dangerous or not, she'd insist he took her with him on the next whale watch. Where did folk go on whale watches? Abroad somewhere, she supposed. The location didn't matter; the mere thought of going on an important mission with Pete made her spine tingle with anticipation. They'd be bound to end up in a relationship together. Her parents would be dubious at first, but he'd win them round. After all, when they saw how happy she was, they couldn't fail to like him.

There were other environmental issues, too, not just whales and beach cleaning. Emma frowned. Hadn't Pete said something about needing to raise the profile of trees, large swathes of rain forest being systematically chopped down and destroyed? And precious little reforestation projects. Now that was worrying!

Emma loved trees. They were her favourite subject to sketch, stark and wind-ravaged in winter and full of leafy blossom in summer – not to mention the beautiful hues of autumn. Yes, she'd be happy if saving trees was their next venture. The wild places were in danger of being lost, Pete was quite right. Not only large swathes of rain forest, either. Too much land was being taken up for building purposes in this country. Yes, folk needed homes to live in, of course they did – preferably eco-friendly homes - but no one was thinking clearly. The planners were all about short term gain, not long-term sustainability.

How had Pete described it? Oh yes, he'd said trees were the lungs of the world and without lungs no one could breathe. All towns and cities needed accessible green space, too. It was criminal the way some children were growing up in concrete jungles, devoid of nature. Another strong gust nearly lifted her off her feet. Steadying herself, Emma scoured her section of the beach with renewed vigour. Suddenly she felt part of this venture.

It wasn't hard to fill her refuse sack. No point doing anything half-heartedly, especially if she wanted Pete to notice her. Or, at least, word to get back to him. Surely, he'd seek out the newbies on return and ask how everyone had got on. It had to be part of the recruitment process. Steadily, she worked her way across the sand. Despite being outside the main tourist season, it was amazing what rubbish was blowing about, or washed up at the shoreline. Amazing what folk left behind, too! She could see the problem. No wonder Pete had been so passionate about it on the doorstep.

Tiring, Emma trudged on, eyes fixed on the ground. Now at the damp edge of the shoreline, she didn't notice the widening gap between herself and the other volunteers.

"Hey, watch out! You need to move, the tide's turning."

Startled by the yell, she felt someone grab her by the arm, dragging her back from the water's edge. Opening her mouth to protest, she gasped as a wave, more powerful than the rest, surged forward and pooled around her boots. The wave behind it, frothing and foaming, looked poised to do the same, if not go further. Alarmed, Emma's heart thudded. The tide really was turning, and fast. How could she not have noticed?

Born and bred in Cornwall, she knew that the sea, whipped by a brisk, in-shore breeze, would race in on a beach as flat as Praa Sands. There was danger here. A fast, incoming tide could easily outstrip a person's normal walking pace.

"Bit cold for a swim – or are you trying to drown yourself?" A fit young man with laughter in his dark eyes caught her free hand. And didn't seem inclined to let go anytime soon. "I've been sent to get you and I think we'd better leg it. How fast can you run?"

Emma needed no second telling. Her boots hampering her progress, she broke into a jog, urged on by the stranger. They had the benefit of the wind behind them now, yet so did the sea. Grateful for the stranger's encouragement, she noticed he didn't let go of her as they fled up the beach, relaxing his grip only as they reached the safety of the high tide mark. It was quite a run! They halted, panting by the seaweed line and she met his gaze, relieved to see that it was open and friendly.

"Thank you." Embarrassed, she cleared her throat, struck by his twinkling brown eyes. Framed by sinfully long lashes, too. And he was looking right at her. "I hope you didn't get wet – by the waves, I mean. I – I'm Emma, by the way. A volunteer. Sorry, new to all this."

"I guessed." He grinned. "Just promise me one thing, Emma. If you do an event like this again, never, ever wander off on your own, or turn your back on the sea. It can be fatal."

Suitably chastened, she nodded, feeling her cheeks flame as he gave her a sexy wink. He sparked her interest. Fumbling with her gloves, she wondered how she could have missed him in the group earlier. Now she felt at a distinct disadvantage – because she'd messed up and made an idiot of herself. He was quite right about the danger. She'd grown up here and shouldn't need telling about the tides. Of course, if Pete had been around, as promised, she wouldn't have needed rescuing. She wouldn't have been on her own.

"I know, honestly, I do." For a moment tears threatened as she realised what could have happened. "Like my Dad says, if there's a tussle, nature always wins. Sorry again. Perhaps I'm not cut out to save the planet."

"Oh, I wouldn't say that." He chuckled, and she saw that he was only a couple of years older than herself. "You've done all right. OK, lecture over. Hi, I'm James."

"Hi." Lost in his dark gaze, she saw that Pete didn't come close to matching James for physique. Somehow, his lean frame didn't fit the role of hero.

The realisation gave her a jolt. They stood a moment, Emma feeling suddenly shy.

"I don't know about you, but I reckon I've done my bit for today." James broke the silence. "This place is freezing. I could murder some fish and chips! How about we sign off with the team leader, then find a café somewhere to thaw out? Just chill for a bit."

Nodding again, Emma swallowed. Telling her to stay where she was, James grinned and reached for her bulging rubbish

sack. Sprinting across the sand with it, he headed towards
the rest of the group. Turning once, he shouted something
over his shoulder that sounded like 'don't move.' As if!
James needn't fret; moving was the last thing on her mind.
Despite the cold, she felt a warm glow. The afternoon was
taking an unexpected upswing.

Watching his retreat, suddenly all Emma could think about
was a smiley, young man with a pair of laughing, brown eyes
that promised fun. Pete's serious face was beginning to fade
from memory. In fact, by comparison he seemed rather dull.
She imagined his earnestness could be rather wearisome
after a while. The wind ruffling her hair, she pulled up the
hood of her anorak which had slipped down during their
mad dash up the beach. Despite thick socks, her toes were
beginning to feel numb. She couldn't wait to find
somewhere warm to thaw out.

Back again, James grabbed her hand. "Right, I've signed us
out. Let's go, Emma."

The little café, trade falling off after the summer season, had
seats to spare. Steering her towards a corner table
overlooking the choppy sea, James grinned.

"You sit, I'll go and order. I think this won't upset anyone's
sensibilities." He pointed to a notice above the counter
stating that all fish sold was from a sustainable source.
"Cod and chips OK? No, don't worry about money. My
invite, this is on me."

The portions were generous. Ravenous after the beach
clean, they both ate quickly, glancing up to exchange smiles
every so often.

"That was delicious. Thank you." Licking her fingers, Emma
giggled. "Now that's two thankyous in one afternoon! Let
me get the coffees."

"A bigger thank you for your company." Shrugging, James

laughed. "Until I was sent to fetch you, the whole thing was becoming rather dull. The fun people weren't there today. At least, I thought they weren't – 'til I met you."

Lingering over coffee, Emma listened while he told her about taking a gap year before going off to uni. A deferred place at Exeter, apparently, to read Maths.

"Ooh, Maths," Emma pulled a face, "my worst subject, I'm afraid. I'm at college doing 'A' Level English and Art. Just started the second year. But my old Art Teacher always said there is a link between Maths and Art. She claimed if a person could do one, no reason they couldn't do the other."

Expecting James to nod politely and return to talking about himself – in her experience, the topic most blokes favoured - she was surprised when he showed interest and wanted to hear more. Tentatively, she shared her dream to become an illustrator and her doubt that she was good enough. Maybe even write and illustrate children's books one day. If she managed reasonable grades, she planned to apply to Plymouth Art College. Now, that was something she'd never told Pete! Even as she spoke, Emma realised that she'd let go of his suggestion to swop subjects. English and Art were a much better fit for her.

"If that's where your passion lies, go for it." Sipping his coffee, James eyed her. "Follow your heart, Emma. So, we're both planning to stay in the West Country. Never been tempted by the Big Smoke?"

Shaking her head, Emma realised that she hadn't. In fact, an opportunity to write children's fiction and hone her artistic skills was all she really aspired to. Oh, and find a nice West Country boy to settle down with.

"Nor me." James gave a slow smile. "Do you believe in fate, Emma? Maybe we were meant to meet. The planets have aligned in our favour. It's mathematical logic! I guess we'd better go in a minute but text me your number. I'd like to see you again."

No, she wanted to say; it's the whales. Their mysterious call from the deep had lured Pete to another land, changing the algorithm. Only James wouldn't understand that.

Another realisation hit: Exeter and Plymouth were not too far apart for a relationship to work. Blushing, she whipped out her mobile phone ready to text him her number. The day had come full circle.

The Snare
Matt Aranson

Tommy "Left-foot beat" had a problem. It started when he was seven, at that fateful tap-dancing lesson he would never forget, not least because his extended family constantly reminded and attempted to shame him for having taken tapping up. He was known then as Tommy Rullo or more commonly as Tom. After this particular lesson, to his complete mortification, his left foot, whether he wished it or not, would tap itself without fail every one and a half seconds. It would do so as he brushed his teeth, put on his clothes, ate his breakfast and whenever Tommy heard music it would do so in time to its beat.

His first worry was what the other kids would say at school. He had already been mocked for choosing tap-dancing as his sport, though Tommy didn't know why as he found tap-dancing genuinely fun. Even Uncle Steven commented "He'd never survive in the army", though unlike at school, Tommy's mother could jump to her son's defence and ask how any seven year old could possibly survive in the army, give Tommy an extra scoop of ice-cream for dinner and tell him that Uncle Steven was just jealous.

The family doctor, Dr. Burns, met with Mrs. Rullo and her son after he received a screaming phone call from Mrs. Rullo about the odd problem. Although chronic foot-tapping was not something which Dr. Burns had ever come across, and he doubted it was a proper medical condition, he agreed to see Mrs. Rullo on good will: one because of the fantastic bake sale she had put on last week in order to raise money for the 24 Ford Street Orphanage, and two because her husband was a gambling partner of Dr. Burns.

Dr. Burns ran Tommy through a series of tests. Tommy's foot tapped with increasing agitation and speed, which distressed his mother more, though Dr. Burns assured her there was no need to worry. At the end of the appointment he took Mrs. Rullo aside and very gently told her that the tests had not shown anything strange, and that perhaps this was just Tommy's way of trying to skive off school, which infuriated Mrs. Rullo as her son would never do something so outrageous.

So Tommy was to be sent back to school, though his mother promised that they would try and find a cure. In the meantime she could not bear to deprive her son of a normal life. This was despite his protests about how his foot would paint him as a moving target for the school bullies, just like the boys who had their hair cut by their mums. Secretly, Tommy wondered if his tapping might put off those who otherwise liked him.

It came very much as a surprise to Tommy that his tapping was actually popular, though he was apprehensive about his new-found fame. It was not the act itself that the other children found interesting but the consistency of it, which during the particularly gruelling parts of the school day, such as the dreaded Wednesday afternoon of double Maths followed by Chemistry, Tommy's tapping became a great distraction to keep the children entertained. Stacy Baker, who was in all of Tommy's classes, had tried to count the number of times his foot had tapped since the 9am bell, and had lost count but boasted she got as far as three thousand, five hundred and seven taps.

Though it didn't last long, at the peak of his popularity, he became the most popular kid in school and hordes would gather around him at lunch time to watch his foot tap in time to the ever faster beat with which the children would sing. "Camptown Races" was a favourite, as was the gauntlet of "She Sells Seashells", which would start slow with all the children singing and end messily with the Blake twins, Gemima and Mariah as the victors, for they were the only children who could sing it at such speed.

It was at school that Tommy earned his nickname "left-foot beat", and it was one that would stick with him as he grew up to be an entertainer and singer. The foot tap became his own personal metronome and was stricter than a snare drum. It continued even as he was in the supermarket or having a cup of coffee. No one had ever recorded a dropped beat.

Tommy had always loved ballads. Out of the records his mother played it was always the sad ones that pulled at his heartstrings. Even before his condition, he had tapped to ballads because he had wanted somehow to capture their essence.

Now half of his repertoire was made up of ballads. They always went down extremely well with the crowd, he could tell by the gentle sobbing coming from the front row and handkerchiefs wiping away tears. Tommy was often taken aback. Had his singing really been that good? They were too kind!

After a particularly successful performance to a crowd of 323 at Knapston Town Hall, Tommy dared to do something he'd never done before - he bought a newspaper, which had the headline "Timmy the Terrific Tapper" and a picture of himself mid-tap, as he was now, though he was also chuckling to himself that they had misprinted his name.

By the side of the review, which Tommy believed had been all too generous, were the audience's comments: "Hilarious", "Witty" and "A satirical genius". It seemed he was well appreciated, but the more he read the more he struggled to find anything about his ballads, even the one which had served as his finale. Not satisfied until he had found at least one comment about the ballads, Tommy continued to read, until he came across, at almost the very bottom of the page "The ending had me in tears…" Here Tommy paused, as his thumb was covering the next line. He anxiously pulled it back to see what else Mrs. Hubert had to say.

They had been tears of laughter. Mrs. Hubert, along with the 322 other members of the crowd, had been laughing at him, and when Tommy realised this he also realised that his ballads were nothing more than a running joke, and he had been the only one not in on it.

Before each song, after each final note and throughout each break the tapping continued. The audience assumed it was part of the act. They could not know, or certainly would not believe, that Tommy had no control over his foot. And when his face contorted as he reached for each high note, pouring his heart into the singing, and his tapping foot grew louder, it was hard not to laugh.

At this moment he wanted nothing more than to shrivel up and hide under the covers of his bed. It was a feeling which he had not felt in such depth since childhood. His memories of that time flooded back. He remembered the first day the tapping had begun, the fear of having to show it to everyone at school. He had only wished that he could be normal like everyone else. Even when he had been accepted by the other kids he knew he had never been understood. He was a novelty back then, as he was now: something that only caught their interest for being different and this might not have been a problem if the world was not constantly throwing up more and newer novelties and was already full of others just like him.

It had taken less than a month for the other kids at school to move on. Instead they gathered around Johnny Parkinson, who was ambidextrous and had what he called a triple-jointed thumb. However what stung Tommy most was not his drop in popularity, which felt like he had been dumped somewhere along a long desert road, no, more than that, it was when the other kids started making fun of him.

He had tried to forget it. To forget being told by classmates that the tapping was annoying or that he should stop trying so hard with it. To forget being told by a teacher that he was a distraction. But his tapping was who he was and despite trying he could not stop it. That was why when his music teacher, Mr. Gerald, one of the few people still impressed by his talent, and a great solace for Tommy, told him he would do well as an entertainer, he had taken it to heart.

But now he was certain this same loss in popularity would repeat itself. And he hated being laughed at for his foot, so, after much deliberation with his wife Gladys, Tommy decided to see a specialist doctor.

The doctor in question was a Mr. Protheroe, who by experimenting in hypnotherapy had successfully cured a dozen patients of their stutters and he convinced Tommy over the phone that the treatment would surely work.

But as Tommy checked the clock in the doctor's surgery, which his leg ticked along to, and as he sat down in the doctor's chair, he wondered if he was making the right choice. Tommy "left-foot beat" was all he had been for a long time, and if he stopped being that, then what would he be? Who would he be?

Yes, the audience had not enjoyed his ballads as he had intended, but they had enjoyed them. And they had never said he was "annoying" or "trying too hard", their reviews were sincere. He was a great performer and here he was about to take away the thing that people liked most about him. Perhaps he had overreacted a little about his career dwindling, and even if it did, would just regular Tommy be able to save it, he wondered. It was all happening too fast, he needed some time to think. But it was just as he had that thought that with the click of the doctor's fingers the hypnotherapy was finished. It was too late to go back. Tommy could only pray that it hadn't worked.

But Tommy's left foot was perfectly still, it was no longer

tapping. When he saw this he wept, wept so hard that even when the doctor exclaimed "I don't believe this!" Tommy did not hear him or realise what had happened. His left foot had stopped tapping, but in its place, his right had started. When Tommy realised this, or rather felt it, his tears turned to laughter and when the doctor asked if he would like to try again with the right, Tommy told him that he was fine the way he was. Tommy "right-foot beat" Rullo exited with a smile.

Killer Parents
Rolande Burrows

My guess is that my parents tried to kill me at least three times.

The thing is, I didn't know it at the time. Okay, I was very small and could well be mis-remembering past events. But as these recollections have been retold and confirmed by my parents and others who were older than me at the time.... I'm certain they are true. Of course, Mum and Dad may not have been motivated to do things deliberately. It just kind of happened.

So this is not a tale of neglect or harsh treatment. It is more a story of my parents 'taking their eye off the ball'... three times!

Yes, that many times (it does make you wonder).

It was in the bath at the age of about nine months that the first incident took place. No, they didn't try to drown me. Too obvious!

And no - I didn't disappear down the plug hole (bizarre idea) which would be quite impossible as I'd been a bonny lad... birth weight 8 lbs and 10oz.

I would have floated well.

It was always bath time on Fridays in our house. A way the relax at the end of a working week. Water was heated in a large gas-heated 'copper' which was filled from our kitchen tap. When the contents were hot enough, the tap at the bottom was opened to allow hot water to flow out and fill the small baby bath on the floor underneath. We all bathed on the kitchen floor. Mum & Dad's bath was a larger tin affair which hung outside on the wall beside the kitchen window. I remember it used to scrape and thump the wall on especially windy days.

So, there I was, sitting up in the warm water playing with the flannel and floating ducks. It seems that whilst my parents' backs were turned, I managed to scoop up the bar of soft soap and somehow swallowed it. Not my most clever action, but then I was still quite young.

I wasn't quite blowing bubbles, but my mother had become hysterical when she saw my lips were turning blue and no amount of Dad's back-slapping was helping. The doctor soon appeared and he grabbed me by the ankles, gave a firm smack and just shook me. Apparently the bar of soap just kind of slipped out.

Good job it did or I wouldn't have been out in my pram for attempt number two.

It was a lovely sunny day and I was being taken for a routine promenade.... being pushed in a huge old pram around Mote Park. We lived in Maidstone and the park was very close to home.

I was a loved child and although I had no siblings, I know that I was wanted and was shown much attention and affection. We didn't have a great deal of money, but I remember being played-with and hearing voices and laughter around me. We lived in my grandmother's cottage, rented from a landlady who apparently brought me a small bag of sweets every time she came to collect the rent. This was exceptionally generous as sugar-rationing was still in force back then.

My cousin Jennifer is eight years older than me. That day, she was babysitting and had been given the task of taking me for this outing in the park. Good fresh air was the thing that every baby needed and although it was Autumn, I would have been wrapped up well.

The thing about this park is the lake. It is quite large and has been witness to many important moments in history. Originally serving as a fresh water source for a Roman villa, it has been home to landed gentry, seen the erection of a couple of grand country mansions and welcomed Sir Winston Churchill in the late 1940s. As a park it has hosted county cricket matches, county fairs, circuses - and still has a boating area, miniature railway and cafe in the midst of huge, wild grassy areas, lawns and woodland. One of England's finest, located in the very heart of the town.

It's role in WW II was at one time as a training ground for allied troops prior to D-Day. My late father (himself a veteran of the North Africa campaign) together with my mother and grandmother (both blitz survivors) had told me stories of those same soldiers. I heard tales that during the war, whilst on a practice manoeuvre, the soldiers had constructed a temporary 'floating' bridge over the water. I believe they were experimenting with a Mulberry Harbour designed structure but it over-turned and threw the men into the lake together with their trucks as they attempted an experimental crossing. I'd heard that many were lost, but military records and period newspapers seem quite vague about that incident, although there are certainly many records of troops being stationed in the park from 1941. Of course the 'Mulberries' had been developed in top secret, to finally serve us well during the Normandy landings.

So, the lake had a reputation for its waters being dark, murky and 'bottomless'. Which cannot really explain my cousin's lapse. Apparently she was pushing me in my pram along one of the many paths beside the water, when she met up with a school friend in the park. Happy times; they were both about eight or nine years old and had plenty to talk about. A little too much perhaps because they hadn't noticed my absence until a man shouted, grabbing my floating pram from the lake and dragging it back up the bank to my cousin.

Saved! .... on this occasion.

But there was yet another trip into Mote Park where my life

was again put at risk.

I was five years old.

The park was zig-zagged by many paths and I was sitting on one of them with the couple of toys I'd been allowed to bring along. Mum and Dad had booked a session with golf club and ball, hired for the pitch & putt course.

Being an 'only child' I was happy to play and I entertained myself in the sunshine and open grassy area of the course. As mum and dad completed a hole, we all moved along a bit. Them teeing-off for the next green and my cars chasing each other along a new section of the path. Now and again my parents looked across to see me, sometimes waved and all went well like this for about 15 minutes. That is, until mum miss-hit a shot. The ball disappeared and mum went off in search. Dad looked up to check on me, only to find that I'd vanished too!

It seems that mum had sliced the ball beautifully and it had hit the only vertical object close by... me! Dad found me poleaxed. I was flat out on the path. By the time mum arrived, I was slowly coming around from the knock-out. It would seem that the sliced ball had smacked me in the head and knocked me clean unconscious. No harm done and I lived the retell the tale. Almost being... well... a hole in one!

It's a wonder I ever made it to adulthood.

I wouldn't say my parents were neglectful and I certainly didn't lack love or attention. But to come so close to death on so many occasions - well I certainly would have to question their parenting skills.

Random Musings
Robert Swann

An unlikely starting place.

Travel is not always exotic and can begin in the most mundane of places; a bus stop for example. It did so for my late father in law who was a man of some substance and gravitas and who was insatiably curious. For the five days a week he donned a fedora and lounge suit eschewing what was, in those days, the accepted uniform of an executive in the city: Pin stripe trousers, a morning jacket, a detached stiff collared shirt and silver-grey tie with pearl tie pin. In his day he was considered avant-garde by his peers. He didn't even carry a furled umbrella – the cad.

Every morning, regularly as clockwork, at precisely the same time he stood at the bus stop waiting to be transported to the local tube station for his journey into Aldwych in the heart of London. Many things happened during his wait for the bus and most of them were predictable: the postman with his bulging sack of mail would labour up and down the suburban garden paths, lightening his load as he progressed; a local school bus would pass by full of students whom he recognised nearly always sat in the same seats - we humans are creatures of habit. His mild OCD caused him to wonder why, in this predictable world, the man who swept the road was inconsistent in his appearances, sometimes coming from a different direction and sometimes not appearing at all or having passed through before his normally allotted time. Unable to contain himself at this inconsistency he approached the road sweeper on a morning when he had arrived a little earlier than usual.

This event took place before the advent of mechanical road sweepers, the operative had a hand pushed cart, a long-handled brush and a broad blade shovel with which to ply his skills. He looked startled at being approached and stopped the humming under his breath of his tune of the moment; this usually being his accompaniment during his solitary daily routine.

"Good morning." My father in law was always extremely polite.

Pausing his task. "Mornin' sir." He touched a forelock and stood back respectfully.

"I have a question for you if you don't mind."

"What would a gent like you want to know from me sir?"

"I am here at the same time every morning with all the others in the bus queue who are also here every morning, but you appear at different times and from different directions. Surely you have a fixed schedule to keep?"

"I do sir, it's a daily schedule and that's exactly why I come from different directions depending on what I believe will happen today that is different from yesterday."

"What could possibly happen today to change your direction of travel?"

"Many things sir." He tilted his cap to the back of his head and scratched his crown. "This morning, like every morning, I listened to the weather forecast. It told me that there will be heavy rain later today, that means that sweeping uphill will be a waste of time."

"Why so?"

"If I sweep uphill and the rain comes down fast it will run down the gutters and take debris to the part I have already swept. That's a waste of time." He resettled his cap square on his head, looking pleased that he had been given the opportunity to discuss his one true passion.

My father in law's irrefutable logic prompted a further question. "That's one reason which I can understand, but your programme is more erratic than would be accounted for by occasional rain. There must be other reasons?"

"There are a lot of other reasons. If the wind blows strong, I don't sweep into it 'cos obviously it will blow the sweepings back behind me, that's another waste of time."

"Fascinating, are there any more reasons?"

"Lots sir." He went through the ritual of the cap and scratching once more. "I don't sweep outside the local schools before the kids get out 'cos if I did, they would make a mess of my cleaning work with their sweetie wrappers and the like."

My father in law finished the sentence for him. "Because that would be a waste of time?"

"Zactly."

"I imagine it's the same with sporting events and Saturday morning pictures and other things like that."

"Zactly," he tapped his temple, in my head I got a timetable of school closing times, special happenings with lots of people making mess. I also know about the weather with wind and rain from day to day. I know when the dustmen are doing their thing, it's no good my sweeping up just before they come. Every morning before I start my work, I think on all of these things and more and I plan my route for that day so that I'm not wasting my time, or the money that you and all the other good people in the bus queue pay for in their cleaning rates." He smiled and picked up his broom again when he saw the bus coming and recommenced his humming ritual.

My father in law reflected on the conversation he had just had. It taught him a salutary lesson. What he had thought of as a mindless job requiring no thought, turned out to require a sophisticated level of forward thinking when carried out by what he came to think of as a professional cleaning man. This was not necessarily the approach taken by all his fellow road sweepers, some of whom would undoubtedly not bother with the subtleties of what they do. But this man had a pride in his work, and it gave him great pleasure to be in control of his job - like the true professional he really was. Later, on the tube train on his way to the office, he compared the philosophy of the road sweeper with some of his fellow city executives and found the same could be applied to them. Some thought ahead and planned for the best possible outcome and others muddled through, not being bothered to give more than the minimum effort. The thought that came to his mind was that the uncommitted followed the axiom that they would do just as little as they could get away with - and keep their jobs, without realising that their employer was paying them just enough to keep them on board, but no more.

The road sweeper who had started off this train of thought was probably unaware of the influence his philosophy had in giving him the fulfilment he obviously enjoyed doing the job that others thought to be mundane and pointless, he very likely didn't consider his approach to be a 'philosophy'. He was happy with his lot and had no intention of 'bettering' himself. Those, unlike him, who do the minimum required to keep their employment, and are consequentially paid just enough to keep them in a job, are often unhappy in their work. Not this man, he found fulfilment in his naturally recurring commitment and clearly reaped the rewards of his dedication.

A salutary lesson for us all (as we consider which of the two philosophies we individually inhabit).

Shared resources and cash problems.

Taking a business flight from Warsaw, Poland, to Lviv, in the Ukraine, with my American business partner – for a first-time visit, I furthered my education both in the air and on the ground. Our aircraft was an Antonov 78, or at least it had been when it left its Russian factory many years before. Numerous repairs later it sat unsteadily on the taxiway waiting for us to board, a hybrid of mismatched parts. Our scant luggage was taken into the cabin and thrown unceremoniously behind the back row of seats in a disorderly heap, together with those of the other passengers.

We took our allotted seats for the short flight, one of us facing forward and one rearward – separated by a rickety wooden table bearing the wounds of passenger abuse. The props began to rotate, slowly at first, then with gathering speed, as the revs increased the whole cabin began to vibrate and shudder. Our empty overhead locker succumbed to the shuddering by springing open and hanging down, swinging back and forth, and we were still on the ground, goodness knows, I thought, what would happen when we got airborne. Once we did, we were looked after by a lone cabin attendant, she was wearing a brown and cream uniform which was clearly several sizes too small and with a hemline much too far above the ground to be decent. She offered us snacks, or at least pointed us in the direction of the refreshments, which were on a tray at the back of the cabin - just in front of the jumbled pile of luggage; the sandwiches looked as untidy as the luggage.

Her body was escaping from several different parts of the uniform which was taut and deformed between the buttons. It was difficult not to stare in fascination at the straining buttons - waiting for them to burst and further to stare at the stain in the shape of Australia central to the left of her somewhat overflowing bosom. She was however very attentive to our needs and with a delightful Eastern European accent she did her best to keep us 'abreast' of the progress of the flight while continually re-latching the errant overhead locker, curtsying oddly as she did so.

The landing was mind focussing, there was a cross wind and the Antonov twitched nervously as we descended crabwise. Finally reaching the ground, first bouncing on the port side wheel and then onto the starboard side one. This wreaked havoc with the overhead locker doors - they opened and shut at random intervals. Finally, as we de-planed, attended to by the sole cabin crew member. I thanked her and asked her to congratulate the pilot and to tell him that he should log all four landings. She looked at me blankly before my meaning dawned on her and she laughed, jiggling her map of Australia stain as she did so.

After our nerve shattering flight, during which we both thought that important items of the aircraft's equipment would be shaken loose with potentially disastrous consequences, we took a taxi to our pre-booked hotel. The hotel was tolerable, but the dining room left much to be desired. Cash was running short, we were deep into our itinerary, and inquiries told us that the banks were shut, and we would be unable to get any local currency, meaning that eating out would not be possible. In those days in places like the Ukraine, credit cards were not operative, so we reconciled ourselves to sampling the limited hotel restaurant fare.

Before partaking of dinner, we decided on a quick walk around town, to blow away the cobwebs and undo the kinks of too much travelling. Our meanderings took us past bars and cafes that were tempting but unavailable because of our lack of local currency. We passed one very inviting restaurant the tables of which were decked with crisp white tablecloths and sparkling silver wear. We looked enviously through the small paned windows at the few people who were enjoying tempting looking meals.

"Look." My business partner pointed to a sticker on one of the windows. It informed us that 'American Express accepted here'

Overjoyed we went in and were shown to our table by a waiter who had a smattering of English, or rather Hollywood American. He and his companions were very attentive, foreign visitors were a rarity all those years ago. After so many bland hotel meals earlier in the visit to Europe, what we enjoyed in this restaurant was a delight for the palate and was accompanied by immoderate quantities of strong local wine. Replete and enjoying coffee and brandy we asked for the bill. It was presented to us with a flourish and was of course in the local currency with which we were not familiar, not having visited the country before.

It was at this point that a serious problem arose. My partner presented his Amex card and the look on the manager's face told us that there was a big problem. It transpired that the Amex card could only be used while the banks were open (this was some time ago) and at this time of night they were firmly in lock-down. There was no possibility of making payment by any other means than cash. We were in a foreign country run by a military dictatorship not known for its leniency in dealing with errant foreigners. By odd Esperanto like words and sign language we conveyed to the manager that we had no local money; he drew on the bottom of the bill the symbols $ and £? Money talks.

We both emptied our pockets and wallets of our paper money which amounted to $24, clearly not enough to pay for the four courses for both of us, with wine, coffee and liqueurs. We were both resigned to being held in a local state police cell (at best) or a military prison at worst, until the banks reopened in the morning. We resigned ourselves to an uncomfortable night in the lockup or possibly worse.

The manager went into a huddle with the waiters and the chef who had joined in the general melee. After a fifteen-minute conflab, and a lot of calculator action, the manager approached us, he slapped the bill down on the table and pointed to what he had written under the local currency total; $14 which, as far as we could interpret, included the service charge. My partner's $20 bill was offered in payment and the international fanned hand signal informed them that they could keep the change. The staff's delight was similar to that which we felt at having enough money to actually pay and give a gratuity and to forego the delights of a night in jail. During a meeting with our client early next morning we recounted the incidence they listened with amusement to our plight and then informed us that we had in one fell swoop broken all local records for gratuities and that the $6 we had offered represented a week's wages for the manager. We concluded our business on the second day of our visit and headed back to the airport to travel on to Moscow. Carrying our own luggage, we walked from the departures building to the same Antonov we had arrived on, the pilot and co-pilot were the same as for the flight here the lone cabin crew member a young blond, clearly, Eastern European young woman was the only change from our inward trip. She attended us well and indicated the same seats that we had occupied before. The disorganised luggage stowage and the overactive overhead locker action was as before.

The only change was the cabin stewardess who at least had a uniform that was the right size, and which didn't stretch between the buttons. It was only later that my partner spotted the tell-tale stain in the shape of Australia on the left bosom but this one was more modest in size and didn't jiggle.

Travelling broadens the mind, it is said, and in this case we learned that having a sumptuous meal for what we considered to be next to nothing and expecting a down at heel airline to have more than one uniform per plane is confirmation that the UK and USA are affluent. We should not judge other countries by our own good fortunes but be mindful of local conditions. When in Rome do as the Romans do.

Musings of a Travelling Man
Robert Swann

Mystery man.

I thought I knew my best man, but it turned out I was embarrassingly ignorant of the real him. Sadly, he died unexpectedly early while working in Belgium. I was asked to give his eulogy at a tiny church in Princes Risborough and gathered information about him from family members. What I uncovered came as a great surprise. I knew him as a golfing partner with whom I socialised; we spent weekends in each other's houses and enjoyed many dinners, glasses of wine and crazy goon-based conversations. But I hardly knew him at all my later researches revealed to me.

I found that my light-hearted friend was a published poet the contents of which work revealed the darker side of his personality, a side I had not known of. In addition to that he came second in a national television cooking competition. He also played guitar as part of his charitable work and appeared at the Royal Albert Hall in front of Princess Alexandra and a few hundred others. As a side-line he wrote songs and music for the Spinners, a popular group at that time who frequently appeared on television.

Arriving early at the tiny church in Princes Risborough to give the eulogy, I checked the position from which I would give the presentation to make sure I could see the congregation and they could see and hear me. To my surprise, the verger placed a lanyard microphone around my neck, there was a surprise in store for me. The church was quaint and held, probably, fifty or so people – hardly requiring the assistance of a microphone. Seeing my puzzled look, he smiled and told me that the sound system was not required for those in the church, but for those congregated outside. He saw I was still puzzled and explained further. It was expected that several hundred people would attend the service and the tiny church could only accommodate a limited number, those who would not fit into the church would be listening al fresco.

There were further surprises in store for me. There was a follow up service to the 'family event' which was held at the Tower of London church and the presentation included letters of condolence from Buckingham Palace and the Archbishop of Canterbury. The incident was a salutary lesson telling me that things are not always what they seem. Mike's life was full to overflowing and he kept it compartmentalised. His lives of Poetry, high church, music and television were kept separate, presumably to allow him to enjoy them all for their individual merits. I sometimes ask myself if there are other things I didn't realise about this remarkable man.

RIP Mike.

Reflections on old age
Ray Dickson

The Pleasures and Social Complexities of Old Age?

My friend gave me a copy of 'Travels with Epicurus - Meditations from a Greek Island on the pleasures of old age'. Perhaps he had listened long enough to my protestations that approaching 79. I still thought like a younger person, but failed to accept the limitations of getting older. I clearly needed an elderly persons training course. I recall my dear father who worked so hard all his life, could not step off the treadmill when he retired. Perhaps I am like him.

But is taking life easier the right approach? So what were the lessons I needed to learn from the Greek philosopher Epicurus? He saw the opportunity of old age as allowing us to focus our brainpower on other matters, often more intimate, cultural and philosophical. Companionship was at the top of Epicurus's list of life's pleasures. He wrote 'Of all the things that wisdom provides to help live one's entire life in happiness, the greatest so far is the possession of friendship'. However, one of Epicurus's prescriptions 'to free oneself from the prison of everyday affairs and politics' – simply does not correspond to what makes many old men and women today genuinely happy.

Looking at humans getting older from a philosophical perspective, we see that only they have a conception of the ageing process. We know when we are born and we know that eventually we will die. Humans can look backward and forwards in time in a way that other animals cannot, and evaluate different stages of their lives in perspective. What does this special human trait mean for the pursuit of happiness and how to flourish in our lives? Knowing oneself can inform our future choices.

There is a debate as to whether ageing necessarily means a decline in health, or whether this is a self-fulfilling prophecy. The problem with this view is that obsolescence is built into our bodies, with cell reproduction slowly declining as we age. Some age-related changes are benign, such as greying hair. Others result in decline in function of the senses and activities of daily life. This is accompanied by an increased susceptibility and frequency of disease, frailty, or disability. In fact, advancing age is the major risk factor for a number of chronic diseases in humans.

The history of ageing has become more confusing because our life-expectancy has skyrocketed in the last century. Only recently has the proportion of the elderly become significant, to the point where their issues have become central to our society, possibly to the detriment of the young. Are there evolutionary benefits to having so many old people around? There isn't nearly such a wide range of ages in other animals, like dogs. The philosophical questions regarding this new stage of life: what is old age for and what role can the elderly play in society? Research has found that as people age, their brains actually improve in many ways, including complex problem-solving and emotional skill abilities.

It can be stated that the ageing population has distinctive qualities which can be used to meet the needs of youth, Older adults are exceptionally suited to meeting these needs in part, because they welcome meaningful, productive activity and engagement. They seek – and need – purpose in their lives. They benefit as well by experiencing emotional satisfaction in relationships with young people. One way to achieve such contact is through volunteer service, which is associated with better physical health and cognitive performance for ageing people.

Volunteer service and the pursuit of cultural hobbies such as music, can make the life of the elderly person personally fulfilling, but increased frailty and not wanting to go out on a cold November evening starts the process of limiting activities. When this happens, a person needs to make his or her own decisions about what brings happiness within their physical constraints.

So what is the effect of an ageing population? The contribution of the elderly has been discussed, but what is the downside. Looking at the figures, the number of people aged over 80 in Britain is forecast to more than double to 6.2 million within the next 25 years.

According to the Office for National Statistics, the number aged over 90 will more than triple, while the number of centenarians will rise almost nine-fold from 13,000 to 111,000, and one in every three children born in England today is likely to live to 100.

With an ageing population with more chronic health conditions, but with new opportunities to live as independently as possible, means the country will have to radically transform how care is delivered outside hospitals. The traditional partitioning of health services – GPs, hospital outpatients, A&E departments, community nurses, emergency mental health care, out of hours units, ambulance services and so on – no longer makes much sense. The reorganisation of the NHS is essential to meet these challenges.

There are also major issues with the provision of social care. Whilst families and savings pay much of social care costs, 47% is paid for by the NHS and local councils. Thus the working population is having to pay towards the costs of an increasingly ageing population.

To conclude, old age is an opportunity to do other activities providing a fulfilling life in later years. But, we cannot escape the health issues inbuilt into bodies and minds, designed from birth with an eventual end date. What would the population of the world be like if nobody died? These health issues have to consider advances in medical science and care which have dramatically increased life expectancy. Most children today, born in the west, have a good chance of living to 100. The social implications are that a smaller percentage of working age people are supporting, to a significant degree, the increasingly elderly population. The country is seeking to minimise its health and care cost by the use of overseas and EU professional labour. The issues are socially complex.

Biographies

Diana Alexander

Diana writes short works of fantasy often inspired by classical stories. Born in Minnesota, she now lives in Washington, D.C., where she spends her days dreaming up worlds and exploring the city.

Anna Barker

Following a successful career as an award-winning feature writer and investigative journalist, Anna published two novels. *The Floating Island* (Arrow, 2008) won a Betty Trask best debut award from the Society of Authors. Her second novel, *Before I Knew Him* (Arrow, 2009) was shortlisted for a Good Housekeeping Good Read award.

Jane Bheemah

Recently, under my pen name Kathryn Haydon, I have been lucky enough to have two books published (by Mezzanotte). The genre is medical romance as befits a retired nurse! "Making the Difference" & "Prognosis Guarded" both have a palliative care backdrop, a specialty I am keen to promote. What better way to do this than craft a story that wraps around your heart – and stays with you long after you finish the book.

Find me on the Mezzanotte website: www.mezzanotte-publishing.co.uk Or follow me on Twitter - @HaydonKathryn Alternatively, check out my Facebook Author Page: Kathryn Haydon @flickypenpot

Emma Childs

Emma is an award-winning professional Artist and illustrator based in South Devon. She exhibits her work on a regular basis throughout the UK, some of her exhibitions to date include Art Monaco in Monte Carlo, Chester and London.

She is perhaps best known for her hand painted Art Deco work which she is commissioned to paint by customers regularly both Nationally and Internationally.

Her painting 'Wake Up' won Art Prize for Gallery 25N's International 'Dreams' exhibition, she also won the Hilder Carter award for her painting 'Poppy Wood'.

www.EmmaChildsArt.co.uk

Nikki Crooks

Nikki is an English Literature student. She has been writing for two years and is overjoyed to be included in her first Anthology.

Liz Diamond

Liz worked as a special needs teacher in an Education Centre attached to a psychiatric hospital before acquiring a two-book deal with Picador. Success was short lived, however, as the first novel didn't get taken up for reviews and she failed to earn out her advance. Since those heady heights she has undertaken counselling training, turned again to writing poetry and has been shortlisted for the Teignmouth Poetry Festival Open Competition twice running. She currently runs workshops in creative writing.

Christine Dodd

Christine's art has been influenced by her career and training as a Carl Jung Psychoanalyst; embodying the world of Jung's research into the behaviour of the human psyche. Christine explores images that spring from the environment and unconscious realms with plein air painting and sketches being her springboard towards a finished piece of art.

Christine paints in oils, acrylics and watercolours. She also has a deep love of Literature, dance and gardening.

Recent exhibitions:

- South West Academy of Fine and Applied Art
- Devon Open Studios
- Harbour House Kingsbridge
- WESC Exeter
- April 2020 Solo Exhibition Totnes
- Showing at Ashburton Gallery, Ashburton

Nicholas Eastwood

1959-62 - Studied Exeter College of Art

1972-2002 - Head and Co-Founder of the Audio-Visual Section (in particular the History of Fine Art Slide Library), University of Exeter New Library.

Lecturer in Contemporary Art to International Students.

June 2002 - Due to growing art commitments both here and abroad, resigned as Head of the Audio-Visual Section, at the University of Exeter New Library, to concentrate on painting and ceramics full-time.

Continued as external lecturer on Contemporary British Art for the English Language Centre, University of Exeter until 2008

Jayne Farleigh

Jayne's journey with painting began at GCSE and A level. She then used her artistic skills in window dressing for some thirteen years, before returning to paint when her first child was born in 2008. Since then she has been attending local art groups, and workshops in Devon, where she has found inspiration and friendship.

The main medium is acrylics, using lots of dry brush technique to build up layers of colour which allow the underpainting to show through.

Jayne sells her work through the South Gate Gallery in Exeter and online internationally.

Nicole Fitton

Nicole is a freelance writer who currently resides in Devon with her family. Her career has spanned three decades working in PR and marketing within Europe and the USA.

Her short stories have been both short and long listed in various competitions and most recently featured on Reflex fiction (May 2019).

As well as a passion for shorts Nicole has published 2 novels - All Tomorrow's Parties, and Forbidden Colours - both of which have received rave reviews. She is currently working on her third novel - a historical thriller set in 1912.

www.nicolefittonauthor.com

Michael Fleming

I've always written. I'm totally hooked. I took a Masters in Creative Writing from 2012 to 2014 and that added a little discipline to the scatter-gun approach I'd taken up to that point. Since then I've written two novels (not placed but marinating) and a novella. However, it's the short story form that grabs me. I've won, been placed or short-listed in a number of competitions including winning the Chelmsford Literary Festival short story prize, the Write Across Sussex short story competition and the Eastbourne Writes competition. I've been placed in others (Charleston, Northampton Writers, Steyning Festival) and short-listed in several including Writers and Artists, Exeter Writers, Yeovil and the H. E. Bates competition.

www.anderidawriterseastbourne.org.uk

Richard Garcka

I am new to writing. Following retirement, I attended Creative Writing classes in Guildford for two years. I am now developing my writing through flash fiction and short stories across a variety of genres and have only recently seen some success in competitions. I have a leaning toward historical fiction and fantasy - any re-imagining of a place or moment in history that we might take for granted.

Christine Genovese

Christine moved to rural Normandy over twenty years ago. How she ended up there is a long story but the change added a rich vein of variety to her writing and life generally.

The culture shock has long ago worn off and she writes about anything that stirs her curiosity. The result is more or less evenly distributed between fiction and non-fiction.

She's had several stories placed in competitions and published in anthologies such as WriteFrance, Sunpenny, Writers Abroad and Ink Tears. Her articles have appeared in The Lady, France Magazine, Thresholds, Walkopedia and Countryside Tales.

Paul Hedge

I live with my wife in Exeter. I am an actor with 'Moonstone Theatre Company'.

In the past I have mainly written stage plays, seven of which were published, and many have been performed, up and down the country. My main writing has concentrated on a fantasy biography, called 'Maurice', and this has been published with Amazon.

Mark Jessett

Mark Jessett is an abstract artist, who makes paintings on paper. He studied Fine Art at Goldsmiths' College and is co-founder of N-E-W Art in Ashburton. He also works as a Paper Consultant with G.F. Smith.

Exploring relationships between colour, surface texture, translucency and opacity, Mark's work is made of simple shapes, underpinned by intricate detail and a distinctive palette. Evocative forms provide the basis for the works, including flag-like shapes and fantasy minerals. Among other interests, Mark draws inspiration from folkloric and educational imagery.

email mark@markjessett.com

Taria Karillion

As the daughter of an antiquarian book dealer, Taria grew up surrounded by far more books than is healthy for one person.

A Literature degree, a journalism course and some gratuitous vocabulary overuse later, her stories have appeared in a Hagrid-sized handful of anthologies, and have won enough literary prizes to fill his other hand. Despite this, she has no need as yet for larger millinery.

Olive Mackintosh-Lowe

Olive Mackintosh-Lowe is a very experienced writer, tutor and creative writing workshop leader based in South London.

She has dedicated seven years to learning about all kinds of writing and storytelling and passing those skills on to children, professionals and aspiring writers.
www.olivelowe.com/about

Colleen MacMahon

Colleen is an actress, writer and painter. She trained at Arts Educational School and subsequently qualified as a Speech and Drama teacher. She has written and directed pieces for theatre groups, had a number of short stories awarded and published and is currently working on her debut novel – the opening chapters of which have recently been shortlisted in two literary competitions. As an artist Colleen specialises in animal and architectural portraiture and illustration, including book covers. She narrates audiobooks.

Trevor Meadows

Email: tpmeadows1964@gmail.com

Ruth Moorey

Ruth is a self-taught Devon artist. In 2017 she was invited to exhibit at Exeter Cathedral. Her silver ink art has proven to be very popular.

Ruth's love of animals is clear. Using acrylics or colouring pencils, she creates fun, soulful, works of art.

Zazzle.co.uk/ruth_moorey_art   @ArtByRuthM

Frank Phillips

Frank Phillips studied graphic design as a young man at Epsom Art School in the 60's. He went on to a career of magazine and book design. His final post was creative art director at BBC books, having had a wonderfully creative and happy working life.

He is a board member of Devon Artists Network.

Christopher Pitman

Chris works predominantly in oils. He is inspired by the coast, estuaries and moors of the Westcountry to which he adds an emotional and expressive element to capture the atmosphere of special moments in time.

He has exhibited extensively, most notably at the South West Academy Open exhibitions 2015, 2016 and 2017 and the winners exhibitions of the SAA Artist of the year 2017 & 2018 at the N.E.C. Birmingham. He has won awards for his art from Teignmouth Art Society, Torbay Guild of Artists, and was a finalist in the SAA Artist of the year 2017 & 2018.

Chris has recently had the honour to be admitted as an Associate of the South West Academy of Fine & Applied Art (SWAc).

www.christopherpitman.co.uk

John Simes

After his career as a teacher and school leader, John Simes founded Collingwood Learning - a consultancy for school improvement. In 2013 he established Collingwood Publishing Limited. John lives with his family in South Devon, England, where he grapples with his addictions to cricket, poetry, and the stunning local landscape, as well as his continuing enthusiasm for education.

A Game of Chess is his second novel and is the sequel to The Dream Factory – published by Matador. You can find out more about John at www.johnsimes.co.uk or follow him on Twitter:@johnthepoet2010.

Wendy Swarbrick

After having a wonderful time teaching physics for more than forty years I embraced the chance to spend time writing fiction. Restless Characters is my attempt to write a ghost story I'd enjoy reading. I write poems, short stories and some longer fiction.